She suddenly broke away from him and ran down the beach.

Turning, she kicked up a spray of the waves that had been washing over their feet. She caught him with a full body splash, and he yelped and laughed with surprise. Then he came after her. She squealed and turned to run, but he tackled her and bore her down to the soft, damp sand.

He leaned over her, looked down into her eyes and then murmured, "Good move. I just saw that goon up on the boardwalk. We are being watched."

He eased closer. "Can I kiss you?"

She tangled her fingers into the richness of his hair, pulling him in, and she kissed him.

UNDERCOVER CONNECTION

New York Times Bestselling Author

HEATHER GRAHAM

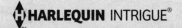

For Lorna Broussard—with love and thanks for all the help and support for…well, many years!

ISBN-13: 978-1-335-63955-4

Recycling programs for this product may not exist in your area.

Undercover Connection

Printed in U.S.A.

www.Harlequin.com

New York Times and *USA TODAY* bestselling author **Heather Graham** has written more than a hundred novels. She's a winner of the Romance Writers of America's Lifetime Achievement Award, a Thriller Writers' Silver Bullet and in 2016, the Thriller Master Award from ITS. She is an active member of International Thriller Writers and Mystery Writers of America, and is the founder of The Slush Pile Players, an author band and theatrical group. An avid scuba diver, ballroom dancer and mother of five, she still enjoys her South Florida home, but also loves to travel.

For more information, check out her website, theoriginalheathergraham.com, or find Heather on Facebook.

Also by Heather Graham

Harlequin Intrigue

Law and Disorder
Shadows in the Night
Out of the Darkness
Undercover Connection

MIRA Books

Echoes of Evil
Pale as Death
Fade to Black
A Dangerous Game
Wicked Deeds
Dark Rites
Dying Breath
A Perfect Obsession
Darkest Journey
Deadly Fate
Haunted Destiny
Flawless

For a complete book list,
visit the author page at Harlequin.com.

CAST OF CHARACTERS

Jasmine Adair—The Miami Dade police officer is undercover in search of a missing friend.

Jorge Fuentes—Jasmine's partner on the police force.

Jacob Wolff—The deep-cover FBI agent is on the tail of a South Beach crime syndicate.

Josef Smirnoff—Kingpin of the Deco Gang, an organized crime group in South Beach.

Victor Kozak—The second-in-command of the Deco gang, who might have designs on the leadership.

Ivan Petrov—Manager of the Gold Sun Club, South Beach's newest hot spot.

Natasha Volkov—She manages all the models for the clubs, making sure the venues are full of beautiful people, and sometimes arranging private engagements.

Mary Ahern—Jasmine's friend is a model, but disappeared while on a job.

Chapter One

The woman on the runway was truly one of the most stunning creatures Jacob Wolff had ever seen. Her skin was pure bronze, as sleek and as dazzling as the deepest sun ray.

When she turned, he could see—even from his distance at the club's bar—that her eyes were light. Green, he thought, and a sharp contrast to her skin. She had amazing hair, long and so shimmering that it was as close to pure black as it was possible to be; so dark it almost had a gleam of violet. She was long-legged, lean and yet exquisitely shaped as she moved in the creation she modeled—a mix of pastel colors that was perfectly enhanced by her skin—the dress was bare at the shoulder and throat with a plunging neckline, and back, and then swept to the floor.

She moved like a woman accustomed to

such a haughty strut: proud, confident, arrogant and perhaps even amused by the awe of the onlookers.

"That one—she will rule the place one day."

Jacob turned.

Ivan Petrov leaned on one elbow across the bar from Jacob. Ivan bartended and—so Jacob believed thus far—ran all things that had to do with the on-the-ground-management of the Gold Sun Club. The burning-hot new establishment was having its grand opening tonight.

"I'd imagine," Jacob said. He leaned closer over the bar and smiled. "And I imagine that she might perhaps be…available?"

Ivan smiled, clearly glad that Jacob had asked him; Ivan was a proud man, appreciative that Jacob had noted his position of power within the club.

"Not…immediately," Ivan said. "She is fairly new. But all things come in good time, my friend, eh? Now you," he said, pouring a shot of vodka for Jacob, "you are fairly new, too. New to Miami Beach—new to our ways. We have our…social…rules, you know."

Jacob knew all too well.

And he knew what happened to those who didn't follow the rules—or who dared to make their own. He'd been south of I-75 that morning, off part of the highway still known as Alligator Alley, and for good reason. He'd been deep in the Everglades where a Seminole ranger had recently discovered a bizarre cache of oil drums, inside of which had been several bodies in various stages of decomposition.

"I have my reputation," Jacob said softly.

Ivan caught Jacob's meaning. Yes, Jacob would follow the rules. But he was his own man—very much a *made* man from the underbelly of New York City. Now, he'd bought a gallery on South Beach; but he'd been doing his other business for years.

At least, that was the information that had been fed to what had become known as the Deco Gang—so called because of the beautifully preserved architecture on South Beach.

Jacob was for all intents and purposes a new major player in the area. And it was important, of course, that he appear to be a team player— but a very powerful team player who respected another man's turf while also keeping a strict hold on his own.

"A man's reputation must be upheld," Ivan said, nodding approvingly.

"While, of course, he gives heed to all that

belongs to another man, as well," Jacob assured him.

A loud clash of drums drew Jacob's attention for a moment. The Dissidents were playing that night; they were supposedly one of the hottest up-and-coming bands, not just in the state, but worldwide.

The grand opening to the Gold Sun Club had been invitation only; tomorrow night, others would flow in, awed by the publicity generated by this celebrity-studded evening. The rich and the beautiful—and the not-so-rich but very beautiful—were all on the ground floor, listening to the popular new band and watching the fashion show.

Jacob took in the place as a whole, noting a balcony level that ran the perimeter, with a bar above the stage. But that night all the guests were downstairs, and Ivan Petrov was manning the main bar himself.

The elegant model on the runway swirled with perfect timing, walking toward the crowd again, pausing to seductively steal a delicious-looking apple from the hands of a pretty boy—a young male model, dressed as Adonis—standing like a statue at the bottom of the steps to the runway.

"I believe," Jacob told Ivan, turning to look at him gravely again, "that my business will be an asset to your business, and that we will work in perfect harmony together."

"Yes," Ivan said. "Mr. Smirnoff invited you, right?"

Jacob nodded. "Josef brought me in."

Ivan said, "He is an important man."

"Yes, I know," Jacob assured him.

If Ivan only knew how.

JASMINE ADAIR—JASMINE ALAMEIN, as far as this group was concerned—was glad that she had managed to learn the art of walking a runway, without tripping, and observing at the same time. It wasn't as if she'd had training or gone to cotillion classes—did they still have cotillion classes?—but she'd been graced with the most wonderful parents in the world.

Her mother had been with the Peace Corps—maybe a natural course for her, having somewhat global roots. Her mom's parents had come from Jordan and Kenya, met and married in Morocco and moved to the United States. Jasmine's mom, Liliana, had been born and grown up in Miami, but had traveled the world to help people before she'd finally settled down. Liliana had been a great mom, always all about kindness to others and passionate that everyone must be careful with others. She had believed that words could make or break a person's day, and truly *seeing* people was one of the most important talents anyone could have in life.

Declan Adair, Jasmine's dad, was mostly Irish-American. He'd been a cop and had taught Jasmine what that meant to him—serving his community.

They had both taught her about absolute equality for every color, race, creed, sex and sexual orientation, and they had both taught her that good people were good people and, all in all, most of the people in the world were good, longing for the same things, especially in America—life, liberty and the pursuit of happiness.

They sounded like a sweet pair of hippies; they had been anything but. Her father had also taught her that those who appeared to be the nicest people in the world often were not— and that lip service didn't mean a hell of a lot and could hide an ocean of lies and misdeeds.

"Judging people—hardest call you'll ever

make," he'd told her once. "Especially when you have to do so quickly."

He'd shaken his head in disgust over the result of a trial often enough, and her mother had always reminded him, "There are things that just aren't allowed before a jury, Declan. Things that the jury just doesn't see and doesn't know."

"Not to worry—we'll get them next time," he would assure her.

Jasmine scanned the crowd. Members of this group, the so-called Deco Gang, hadn't been gotten yet. And they needed to be—no one really knew the full extent of their crimes because they were good. Damned good at knowing how to game the justice system.

Fanatics came in all kinds—and fanatics were dangerous. Just as criminals came in all kinds, and they ruined the lives of those who wanted to live in peace, raising their children, working…enjoying their liberty and pursuing their happiness.

That's why cops were so important—something she had learned when sometimes her dad, the detective, hadn't made it to a birthday party.

Because of him, she'd always wanted to be

a cop. And she was a damned good one, if she did say so herself.

At the moment, it was her mother's training that was paying off. As a child, Jasmine had accompanied her mom to all kinds of fund-raisers—and once she was a teenager, she'd started modeling at fashion shows in order to attract large donations for her mom's various charities. She had worked with a few top designers who were equally passionate about feeding children or raising awareness when natural disasters devastated various regions in the States and around the world.

So as Jasmine strutted and played it up for the audience, she also watched.

The event had attracted the who's who of the city. She could see two television stars who were acting in current hit series. Alphonse Mangiulli—renowned Italian artist—was there, along with Cam Li, the Chinese businessman who had just built two of the largest hotels in the world, one in Dubai and one on Miami Beach. Mathilda Glen—old, old Miami society and money—had made it, along with the famed English film director, Eric Summer.

And amid this gathering of the rich and famous was also a meeting of the loosely organized group of South Beach criminals that the Miami-Dade police called the Deco Gang.

They had come together under the control of a Russian-born kingpin, Josef Smirnoff, and they were an equal-opportunity group of very dangerous criminals. They weren't connected to the Italian Mafia or Cosa Nostra, and they weren't the Asian mob or a cartel from any South American or island country. And they were hard to pin down, using legitimate business for money laundering and for their forays into drug smuggling and dealing and prostitution.

Crimes had been committed; the bodies of victims had been found, but for the most part, those who got in the way of the gang were eliminated. Because of their connections with one another, alibis were abundant, evidence disappeared, and pinning anything on any one individual had been an elusive goal for the police.

Jasmine had used every favor she had saved up to get assigned to this case. It helped that her looks gave her a good cover for infiltration.

Her captain—Mac Lorenzo—probably suspected that she had her own motives. But he didn't ask, and she didn't tell. She hadn't let

Lorenzo know that her personal determination to bring down the Deco Gang had begun when Mary Ahearn had disappeared. Her old friend had vanished without a trace after working with a nightclub that was most probably a front for a very high-scale prostitution ring.

She could see Josef Smirnoff in the front of the crowd; he was smiling and looking right at her. He seemed to like what he saw. Good. He was the man in charge, and she needed access to him. She needed to be able to count his bodyguards and his henchmen and get close to him.

She wasn't working alone; Jasmine was blessed with an incredible partner, Jorge Fuentes.

Along with being a dedicated cop, Jorge was also extremely good-looking, and thanks to that, he'd been given leeway when he'd shown up at the Gold Sun Club, supposedly looking for work. Jasmine had told Natasha Volkov—manager of the models who worked these events or sat about various places looking pretty—that she'd worked with Jorge before and that he was wonderfully easygoing. Turned out the show was short a man; Jorge had been hired on for the day easily. They'd cast him as Adonis and given him a very small costume to wear.

Jorge had been trying to get a moment alone with her as preparations for the fashion show had gone on. Jasmine had been undercover for several weeks prior to the club's opening night, and briefings had been few and far between. The opportunity hadn't arisen as yet, but they'd be able to connect—as soon as the runway show part of the party was over. She was curious what updates Jorge had, but they were both savvy enough to bide their time. Neither of them dared to blow their covers with this group—such a mistake could result in instant death, with neither of them even aware or able to help the other in any way.

Her cover story was complete. She had a rented room on Miami Beach, which she took for a week before answering the ad for models. She'd been given an effective fake résumé—one that showed she'd worked but never been on the top. And might well be hungry to get there.

After a lightning-quick change of clothes backstage, she made another sweep down the runway. She noted the celebrities in attendance. South Beach clubs were like rolls of toilet paper—people used them up and discarded them without a thought. What was popular today might be deserted within a month.

But she didn't think that this enterprise would care—the showy opening was just another front for the illegal activities that kept them going.

She noted the men and women surrounding Josef Smirnoff. He was about six feet tall, big and solidly muscled. His head was immaculately bald, which made his sharp jaw even more prominent and his dark eyes stand out.

On his arm was an up-and-coming young starlet. She was in from California, a lovely blue-eyed blonde, clearly hoping that Smirnoff's connections here would allow her to rub elbows with the right people.

Jasmine hoped that worked out for her— and that she didn't become involved with the wrong people.

Natasha was with him, as well. She had modeled in her own youth, in Europe. About five-eleven and in her midfifties, Natasha had come up through the ranks. One of the girls had whispered to Jasmine that Natasha had always been smart—she had managed to sleep her way up with the right people. She was an attractive woman, keeping her shoulder-length hair a silvery-white color that enhanced her slim features. She kept tight control of the fashion show and other events, and sharp eyes on everyone and everything.

Rumor had it she was sleeping with Josef. It wasn't something she proclaimed or denied. But there were signs. Jasmine wondered if she cared for Josef—or if it was a power play.

Jasmine had to wonder how Natasha felt about the beautiful women who were always around. But she understood, for Natasha, life hadn't been easy. Power probably overrode emotion.

The men by Smirnoff were his immediate bodyguards. Jasmine thought of them as Curly, Moe and Larry. In truth, they were Alejandro Suarez, Antonio Garibaldi and Sasha Antonovich. All three were big men, broad-shouldered and spent their off-hours in the gym. One of the three was always with Smirnoff. On a day like today, they were all close to him.

Victor Kozak was there, as well. Victor was apparently the rising heir to receive control of the action. He was taller and slimmer than Josef, and he had bright blue eyes and perfectly clipped, salt-and-pepper facial hair. He was extremely pleasant to Jasmine—so pleasant that it made her feel uneasy.

She knew about them all somewhat because she had talked to Mary about what she was doing. She had warned Mary that there was suspicion about the group on South Beach that ran so many of the events that called for runway models or beautiful people just to be in a crowd. Beautiful people who, it was rumored, you could engage to spend time with privately. Mary had described many of these players before Jasmine had met them.

Before Mary had disappeared.

The club manager was behind the bar; he didn't often work that kind of labor himself. He usually oversaw what was going on there. He was like the bodyguards—solid, watching, earning his way up the ranks.

Still watching, Jasmine made another of her teasing plays with Jorge—pointing out the next model who was coming down the runway. Kari Anderson was walking along in a black caftan that accented the fairness of her skin and the platinum shimmer of her hair. Jorge stood perfectly still; only his eyes moved, drawing laughter from the crowd.

As Jasmine did her turn around, she noted a

man at the bar. She did not know him, or anything about him. He was a newcomer, Kari had told her. A big man in New York City. He was taller and leaner than any of the other men, and yet Jasmine had the feeling that he was steel-muscled beneath the designer suit he was wearing. He hadn't close-cropped his hair either; it was long, shaggy around his ears, a soft brown.

He was definitely the best looking of the bunch. His face was crafted with sharp clean contours, high defined cheekbones, a nicely squared chin and wide-set, light eyes. He could have been up on the runway, playing "pretty boy" with Jorge.

But of course, newcomer though he might be, he'd be one of "them." He'd recently come to South Beach, pretending to be some kind of an artist and owning and operating a gallery.

The hair. Maybe he believed that would disguise him as an artist—rather than a murdering criminal.

When she had made another turn, after pausing to do a synchronized turn with Kari, she saw that the new guy had left the bar area, along with the bartender. They were near Josef Smirnoff now.

Allowed into the inner circle.

Just as she noticed them, a loud crack rang out. The sound was almost masked by the music.

People didn't react.

Instinct and experience told Jasmine that it was indeed a gunshot. She instantly grabbed hold of Kari and dragged her down to the platform, all but lying over her. Another shot sounded; a light exploded in a hail of sparks. Then the rat-tat-tat of bullets exploded throughout the room.

The crowd began to scream and move.

There was nothing orderly about what happened—people panicked. It was hard not to blame them. It was a fearsome world they lived in.

"Stay down!" Jasmine told Kari, rising carefully.

Jorge was already on the floor, trying to help up a woman who had fallen, in danger of being trampled.

Bodyguards and police hired for the night were trying to bring order. Jasmine jumped into the crowd, trying to fathom where the shots had been fired. It was a light at the end of the runway that had exploded; where the other shot had come from was hard to discern.

The band had panicked, as well. A guitar crashed down on the floor.

Josef Smirnoff was on the ground, too. His bodyguards were near, trying to hold off the people who were set to run over him.

It was an absolute melee.

Jasmine helped up a young man, a white-faced rising star in a new television series. He tried to thank her.

"Get out, go—walk quickly," she said.

There were no more shots. But would they begin again?

She made her way to Smirnoff, ducking beneath the distracted bodyguards. She knelt by him as people raced around her.

"Josef?" she said, reaching for his shoulder, turning him over.

Blood covered his chest. There was no hope for the man; he was already dead, his eyes open in shock. There was blood on her now, blood on the designer gown she'd been wearing, everywhere.

She looked up; Jorge had to be somewhere nearby. Instead she saw a man coming after her, reaching for her as if to attack.

She rolled quickly, avoiding him once. But as she prepared to fight back, she felt as if she had been taken down by a linebacker. She stared up into the eyes of the long-haired newcomer; bright blue eyes, startling against his face and dark hair. She felt his hands on her, felt the strength in his hold.

No. She was going to take him down.

She jackknifed her body, letting him use his own weight against himself, causing him to crash into the floor.

He was obviously surprised. It took him a second—but only a second—to spin himself. He was back on his feet in a hunched position, ready to spring at her.

Where the hell is Jorge?

She feinted as if she would dive down to the left and dived to the right instead. She caught the man with a hard chop to the abdomen that should have stolen his breath.

He didn't give. She was suddenly tackled again, down on the ground, feeling the full power of the man's strength atop her. She stared up into his blue eyes, glistening like ice at the moment.

She realized the crowd was gone; she could

hear the bustle at the doorway, hear the police as they poured in at the entrance.

But right there, at that moment, Josef Smirnoff lay dead in an ungodly pool of blood—blood she wore—just feet away.

And there was this man.

And herself.

"Hey!" Thank God, Jorge had found her. He dived down beside them, as if joining the fight. But he didn't help Jasmine; he made no move against the man. He lay next to her, as if he'd just also been taken down himself.

"Stop! FBI, meet MDPD. Jasmine, he's undercover. Jacob… Jasmine is a cop. My partner," Jorge whispered urgently.

The man couldn't have looked more surprised. Then, he made a play of socking Jorge, and Jorge lay still. The man stood and dragged Jasmine to her feet. For a long moment he looked into her eyes, and then he wrenched her elbow behind her back.

"Play it out," he said, "nothing else to do."

"Sure," Jasmine told him.

And as he led her out—toward Victor Kozak, who now stood in the front, ready to take charge, Jasmine managed to twist and deliver a hard right to his jaw.

He stared at her, rubbing his jaw with his free hand.

"Play it out," she said softly.

The Feds always thought they knew more than the locals, whether they were team people or not. He'd probably be furious. He'd want to call the shots.

But at least his presence meant that the Feds had been aware of this place. They had listened to the police, and they had sent someone in. It was probably what Jorge had been trying to tell her.

Jacob was still staring at her. Well, she did have a damned good right hook.

To her surprise, he almost seemed to smile. "Play it out," he said. And to her continued surprise, he added, "You are one hell of a player!"

Chapter Two

"Someone knew," Jorge said. "Someone knew that Smirnoff came in—that he was selling them all out."

"Maybe," Jacob Wolff said. He was sitting on the sofa in Jasmine's South Beach apartment.

She didn't know why, but it bothered her that he was there. So comfortable. So thoughtful. But it hadn't been until now, with him in her apartment, that she really understood what was going on.

Two weeks ago, Josef Smirnoff had made contact with Dean Jenkins, a special agent assigned to the Miami office. Jenkins had gone to his superiors, and from there, Jacob Wolff had been called in. Among his other talents, he was a linguist, speaking Russian, Ukrainian, Spanish, Portuguese and French, including Cajun and Haitian Creole. He also knew a smattering of Czech and Polish. And German, enough to get by.

Maybe that's why she was resenting him. No one should be that accomplished.

No, it was simply because he had taken her by surprise.

"Maybe someone knew," Wolff said. He added, "And maybe not."

"If not, why—?" Jorge asked.

Wolff leaned forward. "Because," he said softly, "I believe that Kozak set up that hit. Not because he knew about anything that Smirnoff had done, but because he's been planning on taking over. Perhaps for some time.

"Smirnoff came in to us because he was afraid—he'd been the boss forever, but he knew how that could end if a power play went down. He was afraid. He wanted out. Kozak was the one who wanted Smirnoff out. And he figured out how to do it—and make it look as if he was as pure as the driven snow in the whole thing himself. He was visible to dozens of people when Smirnoff was killed. He played his cards right. There were plenty of cops there today, in uniform. What better time to plan an execution, when he wouldn't look the least guilty? In *this* crime ring, he was definitely the next man up—vice president, if you will."

"The thing is, if Kozak figures out something is up, we're all in grave danger," Jorge pointed out. "Undercover may not work."

"Jorge, undercover work is the only thing that might bring them down," Jasmine protested.

She was leaning against the archway between the living-dining area of the apartment and the kitchen. It was late; she was tired. But it had been the first chance for the three of them to talk.

After the chaos, everyone had been interviewed by the police. Stars—the glittering rich and famous and especially the almost-famous—had done endless interviews with the press, as well. Thankfully, there had been plenty of celebrities to garner attention. Jasmine, Jorge and Jacob Wolff had all managed to avoid being seen on television, but still, maintaining their cover had meant they were there for hours.

She'd been desperate to shower, and her blood-soaked gown had gone to the evidence locker.

In the end, they'd been seen leaving together, but that had been all right. Everyone knew that Jorge was Jasmine's friend—she'd brought him into the show, after all.

And as for Jacob Wolff…

"You shouldn't have made that show of going off with us in front of Victor Kozak," she said, glaring at Wolff. She realized her tone was harsh. Too harsh. But this was her apartment—or, at least, her cover persona's apartment—and she felt like a cat on a hot tin roof while he relaxed comfortably on her rented couch.

She needed to take a deep breath; start over with the agent.

He didn't look her way, just shrugged. "I told Ivan, the bartender, I wanted to get to know you. They believe I'm an important player out of New York. Right now, they're observing me. And they believe if they respect me, I'll respect them, play by their rules. I'm supposed to be a money launderer—I'm not into many of their criminal activities, including prostitution or any form of modern slavery. My cover is that of an art dealer with dozens of foreign ties.

"Before all this went down tonight, I was trying to befriend Ivan, who apparently manages the girls. I'm trying to figure out how the women are entangled in their web. Apparently, they move slowly. Most probably, with drugs. Before all this went down tonight, I'd asked about you, Jasmine, as if taking advantage of the 'friendship' they'll offer me. He said you weren't available yet, but that all good things come in time, or something to that effect. He'll think I took advantage of the situation instead—and that I'm offering you all the comfort a man in my position can offer."

"Really?" Jasmine asked. "But I was with Jorge."

Wolff finally looked at her, waving a hand in the air. "Yes, and they all know you two are friends, and that it's normal you would have left with Jorge. But Jorge is gay."

"That's what you told them?" Jasmine asked.

"I am gay," Jorge said, shrugging.

Jasmine turned to him. "You are? You never told me."

"You never asked. Hey, we're great partners. I never asked who you were dating. Oh, wait, you never do seem to date."

Jasmine could have kicked him. "Hey!" she protested. Great. She felt like an idiot. She and Jorge were close, but…it was true. They'd been working together for a while, they were friends. Just friends. And because of that, she hadn't thought to ask—

It didn't matter. They'd both tacitly known from the beginning as partners they'd never date each other, and neither had ever thought to ask the other about their love life.

She had to draw some dignity out of this situation.

"At least we did the expected," she said. "I guarantee we were watched. Oh, and by the way, Ivan Petrov controls the venue. But Natasha really runs the models. She gives the assignments, and she's the one who hands out the paychecks."

Wolff looked at her. "You're going to have to be very careful. From all that I've been told, she's been with this enterprise from the beginning. She may be almost as powerful as Kozak himself. When Natasha got into it, she wasn't manipulated into sex work. She used sex as an investment. She came into it as a model, slept with whomever they wanted—and worked her way up to Kozak."

"I am careful," Jasmine told him. "I'm a good cop—determined, but not suicidal."

"I'm glad to hear it. So, this is all as good as it can be," Wolff said, shaking his head.

"What matters most here tonight is that we've lost Smirnoff, our informant. And we've still got to somehow get into this and take them all down. We have to take Kozak down, with all the budding lieutenants, too. My position with this group is pretty solid—the Bureau does an amazing job when it comes to inventing a history. But the fashion show is over. The opening is over. The club will be closed down for a few days."

"I'll have an in, don't worry. The last words from Natasha this evening had to do with us all reporting in tomorrow—for one, to return the clothing. For another, to find out where we go from here." Jasmine hesitated.

"They haven't asked you to entertain anyone yet?" Wolff asked.

"New girls get a chance to believe they're just models. After that, they're asked to escort at certain times, and, of course, from there…"

"We'll have this wrapped up before then," Jorge assured her.

"And if not, you'll just get the hell out of it," Wolff said.

"You don't have to be protective. I've been with the Special Investigations Division for three years now, and I've dealt with some pretty heinous people," Jasmine told him.

"I've dealt with them, too," Wolff said quietly. "And I spent this afternoon up in the Everglades, a plot of godforsaken swamp with a bunch of oil drums filled with bodies. And I've been FBI for almost a decade. That didn't make today any better."

"I'm not saying anything makes it better. I'm just saying I can take care of myself," Jasmine said.

She really hadn't meant to be argumentative. But she did know what she was doing, and throughout her career, she'd learned it was usually the people who felt the need to emphasize their competency who were the ones who weren't so sure of their competency after all. She was confident in her abilities—or, at least she had thought she was.

With this Fed, she was becoming defensive. She hated the feeling.

"Guys, guys! Time-out," Jorge said.

Wolff stood, apparently all but dismissing her. "I'm heading back to my place. Most days, I'll be hanging around a real art shop that's supposedly mine. Dolphin Galleries."

He handed Jorge a card, then turned to look

at Jasmine. "Feel free to watch out for me. In my mind, no one cop can beat everything out there. We all need people watching our backs. I'm more than happy to know I have MDPD in deep with me."

His words didn't help in the least; Jasmine still felt like a chastised toddler. What made it worse was the fact he was right. They did need to look out for one another.

She wanted to apologize. They had met awkwardly. She wasn't brash, she wasn't an idiot— she was a team player. But despite his words, she had the sense that he was already doubting her.

"I'll be hanging as close as I can," he said. "The woman managing the shop, Katrina Partridge, is with us. If you need me and I'm not there, just ask her. I trust her with my life."

He didn't look back. If he had done so, Jasmine was certain, it would have been to look at Jorge with pity for having been paired with her.

When Jacob was gone, she strode to the door and slid the bolts. She had three.

"Jerk!" she said. She turned back into the room and flounced down on the sofa.

"Not really. Just bad circumstances," Jorge

said, taking a seat beside her. "I, uh, actually like the guy."

She looked at him. "I don't dislike him. I don't really know him."

"Could have fooled me."

She ignored that. "Jorge, how did it happen? We were all there. The place was spilling over with cops. And someone shot and killed Smirnoff—with all of us there—and we don't know who or how."

"They were counting on the place being filled with cops, Jasmine. Detectives will be on the case and our crime scene techs will find a trajectory for the bullet that killed him. We do our part, they do theirs. Thing is, whoever killed him, they were just the working part of the bigger machine. We have to get to the major players—Kozak, whoever else. Not that the man or woman who was pulling the trigger shouldn't serve life, but…it won't matter."

"No, it won't matter," she agreed. What they needed to do was find Mary. She nodded.

He took her hand and squeezed it. "You're just thrown. We weren't expecting to take them all down tonight."

"We weren't expecting Smirnoff to get

killed tonight. I—I didn't even know he'd gone to the FBI!"

"I knew but couldn't tell you. And I didn't know that Smirnoff would be killed before I had a chance to loop you in. I'm sorry—I put you and Wolff both in a bad position. At least you didn't shoot each other. You know you're resenting him because he had you down."

"He did not have me down."

"Almost had you down."

"I almost had him down."

"Ouch. Take a breath," Jorge warned.

She did, and she shook her head. "I worked with a Fed once."

"And he was okay, right? Come on, we're all going in the same direction."

"He was great. Old dude—kept telling me he had a granddaughter my age. Made me feel like I should have been in bed by ten," Jasmine said and smiled.

Jorge arched his brow at her.

"Okay, okay," she said. "I resent the fact he almost had me down. But really, I almost had him, too." She squeezed his hand in return. "How come we never have discussed our love lives and this stranger knew more about you than I did?"

"'Cause neither of us cares what our preferences are, and we work well together—and we enjoy what we're doing. And Wolff for sure had all of us checked out before agreeing to work with us. He'd need to know our backgrounds and that we're clean cops. Also, you're a workaholic and even when we're grabbing quick food or popping into a bookstore, we're still working."

"Not really," she told him. "Honestly, not until this operation."

He nodded. "Mary," he said softly.

"Jorge, I'm so afraid she's dead." She paused. "Even more now. Do you have any details about the oil drums they found today? All I've seen is what has been on the news. Captain Lorenzo was even with the cops doing the interviews at the show, but I didn't get to ask him anything. Obviously, I did my best to be a near hysterical model."

"You were terrific."

She laughed. "So were you." Jasmine tried to smile, but she was searching out his eyes.

"Mary wasn't in one of the oil drums," he said.

"You're sure?"

"Positive. The bodies discovered were all men."

"Oh, thank God. I mean… I'm not glad that anyone was dead, but—"

"It's all right," Jorge assured her. "I understand. So, tomorrow will be tense. I'm going to get out of here. Let you get some sleep." He started to rise, and then he didn't. "Never mind."

"Never mind?"

"I'm going to stay here."

"I don't need to be protected," she said. "Bolts on the door, gun next to the bed."

"You don't need to be protected?" Jorge said. "I do! Safety in numbers. Bolt the door and let's get some sleep."

She rose. "Okay, I lied, and you're right—anyone can be taken by surprise. And I have been a jerk and I don't know why."

"I do," Jorge said softly. "You really shouldn't be working this case. You have a personal involvement. And in a way, so do I. I've met Mary."

Jasmine nodded. "I don't feel that I'm really up to speed yet, despite what we learned from Wolff. I'll get you some pillows and bedding," she told him.

"What time are we supposed to be where?" he asked her as she laid out sheets on the sofa.

"Ten o'clock, back at the club."

"I'm willing to bet half of it will still be shut down."

"We won't be going to the floor. We'll be picking up our pay in the offices, using the VIP entrance on the side to the green room and staging areas."

"You know that we can get in?"

She nodded. "I wound up with Natasha and the other girls in a little group when the police were herding people for interviews. Natasha asked the lead detective—Detective Greenberg is in charge for the City of Miami Beach—and he told her that they'd cordon off the club area until they finished with the investigation. Owners and operators were free to use the building where the police weren't investigating."

"Then go to bed. We'll begin again in the morning."

Jorge was clearly thinking something but not saying it.

"What?" she pressed.

"I didn't know until today that the FBI was in on this case—the briefing was why I arrived late. MDPD found the group operating the Gold Sun Club to be shady, as did the cops with the City of Miami Beach. But there's been no hard evidence against them and nothing that anyone could do. I know you've been talking to Captain Lorenzo about them for a while, but…we just found out today that Smirnoff was about to give evidence against the whole shebang. I'm just—"

"Just what?"

He grimaced. "I like the Feds. They have more resources than we do. They have more reach across state lines. Across international lines. And I don't know how long I'll get to be one of the models—if the big show ended in disaster, I could be out fast. And then I won't be around to help you."

"I'm willing to bet the Deco Gang will keep planning. Kozak will say that all the people who had been hired for jobs at the club will still need work. He'll go forward in Smirnoff's name—Smirnoff would not want to have been frightened off Miami Beach. We'll be in."

"You will be. I may not. So, I'm just glad that…well, that there's another law enforcement agent undercover on this case. Speaking of undercover…" Jorge grabbed his blanket and turned around, smiling as he feigned sleep.

Jasmine opened her mouth to speak. She

shook her head and went to the bedroom. Ready for bed and curled up, she admitted to herself that she just might be glad for Jacob Wolff's involvement, too.

She had assumed the group was trading in prostitution, turning models into drug addicts and then trafficking them.

She hadn't known about the bodies in the barrels. And she hadn't suspected that Smirnoff was going to die.

So she was glad she would have backup if she had to continue getting close to these dangerous players. Otherwise she probably should back right out of the case.

Except she just couldn't. They had Mary. They had her somewhere.

And Jasmine had to pray her friend was still alive.

Chapter Three

Jacob could remember coming to South Beach with his parents as a child. Back then, the gentrification of the area was already underway.

His mom liked to tell him about the way it had been when she had been young, when the world had yet to realize the beauty and architectural value of the art deco hotels—and when the young and beautiful had headed north on South Beach to the fabulous Fontainebleau and other such hotels where the likes of Sinatra and others had performed. In her day, there had been tons of bagel shops, and high school kids had all come to hang out by the water with their surfboards—despite a lack of anything that resembled real surf.

It was where his parents had met. His father had once told him, not without some humor, that he'd fallen in love over a twenty-five-cent bagel.

The beach was beautiful. Jacob had opted for a little boutique hotel right on the water. Fisher House had been built in the early 1920s when a great deal around it had been nothing but scrub, brush and palms. It had been completely renovated and revamped about a decade ago and was charming, intimate and historic, filled with framed pictures of long ago. The back door opened to a vast porch—half filled with dining tables—and then a tiled path led to the pool and beyond down to the ocean.

Jacob started the morning early, out on the sand, watching the sun come up, feeling the ocean breeze and listening to the seagulls cry. The rising sun was shining down on the water, creating a sparkling scene with diamond-like bits of brilliance all around him.

It was a piece of heaven. Sand between his toes, and then a quick dip in the water—cool and yet temperate in the early-morning hour. He loved it. Home for him in the last few years had been Washington, D.C., or New York City. There were beaches to be found, yes, but nothing like this. So, for the first hour of the day, he let himself just love the feel of salt air around him, hear the lulling rush of waves and look out over the endless water.

There was nothing like seeing it like a native. By 9:00 a.m., he was heading along Ocean Drive. The city was coming alive by then; roller skaters whizzed by him and traffic was heavy. Art galleries and shops were beginning to open, and tourists were flocking out in all manner of beach apparel, some wearing scanty clothing and some not. While most American men were fond of surf shorts for dipping in the water, Europeans tended to Speedos and as little on their bodies as possible. It was a generalization; he didn't like generalizations, but in this case, he was pretty sure he was right.

A fellow with a belly that surely hid his toes from his own sight—and his Speedo—walked on by and greeted Jacob with a cheerful "good morning" that was spoken with a heavy foreign accent.

Jacob smiled. The man was happy with himself and within the legal bounds of propriety for this section of the beach. And that was what mattered.

He stopped into the News Café. It was a

great place to see…and be seen. Before he'd been murdered, the famous designer Gianni Versace had lived in one of South Beach's grand old mansions. He had also dined many a morning at the News Café. Tourists flocked there. So did locals.

Jacob picked up a newspaper, ordered an egg dish and sat back and watched—and listened.

The conversation was all about the shooting of Josef Smirnoff at what should have been one of the brightest moments in the pseudo-plastic environment of the beach.

"You can bring in all the stars you want— but with *those* people—"

"I heard it was a mob hit!"

"Did you know that earlier, like in the morning, three bodies were found in oil drums out in the Everglades?"

"Yeah. I don't think anyone had even reported them missing. No ID's as of yet, but hey…like we don't have enough problems down here."

People were talking. Naturally.

"Told you we shouldn't have come to Miami."

"Hey, mobsters kill mobsters. No one else

was injured. Bunch of shots, from what I read, but only the mobster was killed."

Someone who was apparently a local spoke up.

"Actually, honestly, we're not that bad a city. I mean, my dad says that most of our bad crimes are committed by out-of-towners and not our population."

Bad crimes… Sure, like most people in the world, locals here wanted to fall in love, buy houses, raise children and seek the best lives possible.

But it was true, too, that South Florida was one massive melting pot—perhaps like New York City in the last decade. People came from all the Caribbean islands, Central and South America, the countries that had once comprised the Soviet Union, and from all over the world.

Most came in pursuit of a new life and freedom. Some came because a melting pot was simply a good place for criminal activity.

While he people-watched, Jacob replayed everything he had seen the day before in his mind. He remembered what he had heard.

Witnesses hadn't been lying or overly rattled when they had reported that it seemed the shots had come from all over. From the bar, he'd had a good place to observe the whole room. And then, as Ivan had muttered that they could go closer and see, they had done so.

The shooter hadn't been close to Josef Smirnoff—Jacob had been near him and if someone had shot him from up close, he'd have known.

He was pretty sure that the shooters had been stationed in the alcoves on the balcony that surrounded the ground floor, just outside the offices and private rooms on the second floor. The space allowed for customers to enjoy a band from upstairs, without being in the crowd below.

When he'd looked up at the balconies earlier, he hadn't seen anyone on them. The stairs might have been blocked.

Would Jasmine have known that detail? Or would they have shared that information with a new girl?

Jasmine had, beyond a doubt, drawn attention last night. She had been captivatingly beautiful, and she had played the runway perfectly, austere and yet with a sense of fun. She was perfect for the role she was playing.

The band, the models, the excitement... It had all been perfect for the setup. It was really a miracle that no one else had been hit.

He had thought that Jasmine was going after Josef Smirnoff when he had seen her lunge at him—getting close to see that the deed was done, that he was finished off if the bullets hadn't done their work. He'd never forget her surprise when he had tackled her...

Nor his own shock when she had thrown him off.

He was surprised to find himself smiling—he wasn't often taken unaware. Then again, while he'd known that MDPD had police officers working undercover, he hadn't been informed that one of them was working the runway.

A dangerous place.

But she worked it well. She had an in he could never have.

He pictured it all in his mind again. There had been multiple shooters but only one target—Josef Smirnoff. Create panic, and it might well have appeared that Smirnoff had been killed in a rain of bullets that could have been meant for anyone.

Jacob paid his bill and headed out, walking

toward Dolphin Galleries. He felt the burner phone in his left pocket vibrate and he quickly pulled it out. Dean Jenkins, his Miami office counterpart, was calling.

"You alone?"

The street was busy, but as Jacob walked, he was well aware that by "alone," Dean was asking if he was far from those involved with the Deco Gang.

"I am," he said.

"They're doing the autopsy now. Someone apparently had a bead on the bastard's heart. It's amazing that no one else was hurt. Oh, beyond cuts and bruises, I mean. People trampled people. But the bullets that didn't hit Smirnoff hit the walls."

"They only wanted Smirnoff dead. Kill a mobster, and the police might not look so hard. Kill a pretty ingenue, a pop star or a music icon, and the heat never ends."

"Yep. I wanted to let you know that I'm on the ground with the detective from the City of Miami Beach and another guy from Miami-Dade PD. Figured if I was around asking questions I'd be in close contact, and you could act annoyed and harassed."

"Good."

"You met the undercover Miami-Dade cops, right?" Dean asked.

"I did. We've talked."

"Good. The powers that be are stressing communication. They don't want any of you ending up in the swamp."

"Good to hear. I don't think I'd fit into an oil drum. Don't worry, we've got each other's backs."

"Have you been asked to move any money for the organization yet?"

"On my way in to the gallery now," Jacob said. "I expect I'll see someone soon enough."

"It may take some time, with that murder at the club last night, you know."

"A murder that I think they planned. I'd bet they'll contact me today."

"You're on. Keep up with MDPD, all right? Word from the top. Both the cops and our agency are accustomed to undercover operations, but this one is more than dicey."

"At least I get to bathe for this one," Jacob told him.

"There's a bright spot to everything, huh?"

"You bet."

He ended the call, slid the phone back in his pocket and headed toward the gallery.

The sun was shining overhead. People were out on the beach, playing, soaking up the heat. The shadow of last night's murder couldn't ruin a vacation for the visitors who had planned for an entire year.

Besides, it was a shady rich man, a mobster, who had been killed.

He who lives by the sword...

Jacob turned the corner. Ivan Petrov was standing in front of the gallery, studying a piece of modern art.

MOE, CURLY AND LARRY—or, rather Alejandro Suarez, Antonio Garibaldi and Sasha Antonovich—were upstairs when Jasmine arrived with Jorge at precisely 10:00 a.m. the next day.

Alejandro was at the top of the stairs. Sasha was at the door to what had once been Josef Smirnoff's office and was now the throne room for Victor Kozak.

Jasmine had made a point of greeting both Alejandro and Sasha. She presumed that Antonio was in the room with Victor, which he was. She saw him when the door to that inner sanctum opened and Natasha Volkov walked out.

The door immediately shut behind her, but

not before Jasmine could see that Victor Kozak was seated at what had been Josef Smirnoff's desk.

The king is dead; long live the king, she thought.

This had shades of all kinds of Shakespearean tragedy on it. Apparently, Josef Smirnoff had known that someone had been planning to kill him—he just hadn't known who. Maybe he had suspected Kozak but not known. And he probably hadn't imagined that he'd be gunned down at the celebrity opening for the club.

She knew that Smirnoff hadn't exactly been a good man. She had heard, though, that he wasn't on the truly evil side of bad. He'd preferred strong-arm tactics to murder. He'd rather have his debts paid, and how did a dead man pay a debt?

Jasmine couldn't defend Smirnoff. However, she believed that Kozak was purely evil. It made her skin crawl to be near him. She had a feeling he'd kill his own mother if he saw it as a good career move.

"Ah, you are here! Such a good girl," Natasha said, slipping an arm around Jasmine's shoulder and moving her down the hallway.

She turned back to Jorge. "You come, too, pretty boy. You are a good boy, too."

Jorge smiled.

Natasha opened the door into a giant closet– dressing room combo. There were racks of clothing and rows of tables with mirrors surrounded by bright lights for the girls to use. Before the show the day before, the room had been filled with dressers, stylists and makeup artists.

"So sad. Poor Josef," Natasha said, admitting them through the door and then closing it. She made a display of bringing her fingers to her eyes, as if she'd been crying. Her face was not, however, tearstained.

"We are all in shock, in mourning today," Natasha added. "So, let me pay you for last night and we will talk for a minute, yes? Maybe you can help."

"Definitely," Jasmine said. "Talking would be good. Mr. Smirnoff was so kind to all of us. It's so horrible what happened."

"Terrible," Jorge agreed.

"So." Natasha grabbed a large manila envelope off one of the dressers and took out a sizable wad of cash. She counted off the amount for each of their fees. When Natasha casually handed it over, Jasmine saw it was all in large bills. It seemed like a lot of cash to have lying around.

Natasha indicated a grouping of leather love seats and chairs where models and performers waited once their makeup was complete.

Jorge and Jasmine took chairs.

"You—you were very brave," she said, looking at Jasmine. "I was behind the curtain, but I saw the way you protected Kari and tried to help poor Josef."

"Oh, no, not so brave," Jasmine said. "When I was a child… I was with my parents in the Middle East, and my father taught me to get down, and get everyone around me down, anytime I heard gunshots. It was just instinct."

"I tried to get to Jasmine," Jorge said, "because she's my friend."

"Of course, of course," Natasha said. "But you two and Kari were the ones who were out on the runway when it all happened. What did you see? Of course, I know that the police talked to everyone last night, but…we're so upset about Josef! Perhaps you've remembered something…something that you might have seen?"

Jasmine shook her head. "Oh, Natasha. This

is terrible, but I was only thinking about saving myself at first. I didn't see anything at all." Jasmine wished that she wasn't lying. She could easily be passionate because her words were true. She wished to hell that she had seen something—anything.

She had just heard the bullets flying. And seen Josef Smirnoff go down.

"I'm so, so sorry," she said. "Of course, I suppose this means that… Well, if you need anything from me in the future, I'd be so happy to work with you again."

Natasha smiled. "Jasmine, you must not worry. We will always have a need for you. We are a loyal family here! And, Jorge, of course, you, too."

"Thank you," Jorge said earnestly.

"But nothing—nothing at all?" Natasha persisted. "Tell me about your night, from the time you stepped out on the runway."

"It was so wonderful!" Jasmine said. "At first, I could hear the crowd. We were having a great time on the runway, and I heard people laughing and having fun…and then, that sound! I didn't realize at first that I was hearing bullets. And then…then it was as if I knew instantly. My past, maybe," she whispered. "And I went for Kari, and when I saw Josef down on the floor, I wanted to help… He'd been good to me, you know? Then that man—a friend of Josef's, I think—thought that I was trying to hurt Josef, and he…he tackled me."

"And you were angry, of course," Natasha murmured.

"Well, at first, of course, but it was okay after. He apologized to me. He told me he thought that I wanted to hurt Josef. He was very sincere. So apologetic."

"He saw to it that we got back to Jasmine's place safely. I liked him," Jorge said.

"And you, Jasmine? Did you like him?" Natasha asked.

"After we talked, of course. He was very apologetic. He told me that he's new to Miami Beach—new to Miami. He was working up north, but he got tired of snow and ice and had some connections to help him start up in business down here, and so…he was sad that his first time really heading to a fine event ended so tragically."

"So. He made moves on you," Natasha said softly. She wasn't pleased, and Jasmine recognized why.

Jasmine was now a commodity—one controlled by Natasha—even if she wasn't supposed to really understand that yet. This newcomer needed to go through Natasha—her and Victor Kozak now—if he wanted to have Jasmine as his own special escort.

"Oh, no, he didn't make moves," Jasmine said.

"He was a gentleman. Almost as if he was one of your security people. He just saw that we got home safely," Jorge said. He looked at Jasmine. "I thought maybe he liked me better."

"Oh?" Natasha said. "Interesting."

"No, no, Jorge—he didn't like you better!" Jasmine said. She knew that Jorge was smirking inwardly, and yet he was playing it well. They were both saying the right things in order to be able to stay close with Jacob as they ventured further into the world of Deco Gang.

They needed everyone in on this—Federal and local. Jorge had been right.

"You found him to be a nice man?" Natasha asked.

"Very," Jorge said before Jasmine could answer.

"Jorge, I am sorry, I don't think that he's interested in you," Natasha said. "He did express interest in Jasmine. But we shall see. Be nice to him, if he should see you or try to contact you. But if he does so, you must let me know right away."

"Of course," Jasmine said, eyes wide. "I know that you'll watch out for me."

"Yes, of course. We will watch out for you," Natasha said. She smiled. "We are family here. So, now, come with me. There will be another event soon enough. We will mourn Josef, of course. But so many are dependent on us for a living, we cannot stop. We will have a memorial or something this weekend on the beach. You will be part of it. We are family, yes? We don't let our people…down. For now, you will give Victor Kozak your…condolences."

Give him their condolences. If this had been happening just years earlier, they might well have been expected to kneel and kiss Kozak's ring.

She and Jorge both smiled naively. "Definitely," Jasmine said.

They rose; Jasmine led them down the hall.

Antonio and Alejandro were by the door to the office. Jasmine knew that Sasha Antonovich had to still be guarding the door.

Natasha tapped on the door to the office. Kozak called out, "Come in," and they entered.

He was alone, poring over papers that lay on the table before him.

"We're so sorry for your loss," Jasmine ventured timidly when Kozak didn't look up.

"The police are still in the club downstairs," he said, shaking his head. "They want to know about the balconies. I want to help them. I want to find the person who did this to our beloved Josef. But the balconies were closed off. Just with velvet cords, of course, but… Ah, Jasmine! We were all so enchanted with your performance," he said, looking up. "And you, too, of course. You were the perfect foil for the girls," he told Jorge.

"Thank you," Jorge murmured.

"I don't know who was on the balcony," Victor went on. "We'd said there would be no one on the balcony."

"Maybe the police have ways to find out," Jorge suggested in a hopeful voice.

Victor Kozak waved a hand in the air. "Maybe, maybe not. We'll keep up our own line of questioning. Anyway…"

He seemed to stop in midthought and gave his attention to them. "Please, I know that you were hired by Josef, but…it is my sincere hope that you will remain with us. We pay our regular models a retainer, which you will receive while we wait for this…for this painful situation to be behind us. That is, if you still wish to be with us."

"For sure!" Jasmine said.

"Retainer? Me, too?" Jorge asked hopefully.

Kozak glanced over at Natasha. She must have given him her approval with the slightest nod.

"Yes, you were quite the centerpiece for our lovely young girls. We have a reputation for always having beautiful people in our clubs. All you need to do is be around, available to us, and maybe meet some people we'd like to introduce you to. Please, we will be in touch. You may come in tomorrow for your paychecks."

They both thanked him profusely. Natasha led them down to the street.

As they were going out, Kari Anderson was just arriving. She threw her arms around Jasmine, shaking.

"I don't think I had a chance to thank you. You saved my life!" Kari told her.

"Kari, I just made you get down," Jasmine said, flushing and very aware that both Natasha and Sasha were watching the exchange.

"Instinct!" she added quickly. "And we're all just so lucky...except for poor Josef."

"I know, it's so terrible," said the young blonde, her empathy real. Jasmine liked Kari. She was an honest kind person who seemed oblivious to her natural beauty. "Josef was always nice. It's so sad. Terrible that people do these things today! Terrible that poor Josef was caught in it all."

Naive—just like Mary, Jasmine thought. Not lacking confidence but unaware of just how much they had to offer.

"Come on up. We will straighten all out with you, Kari," Natasha said. "We will be all right. Victor will see to it," she added. "Now, you two run along and try to enjoy some downtime. Kari, come with me. We will have work for all of you—you needn't stress."

"See you, Kari," Jorge said, waving.

He and Jasmine started down the street while Natasha led Kari past Sasha and up the stairs.

"I worry about her," Jasmine said.

"I worry about all of us," Jorge said. "I was worried about the two of us unarmed during the show. We were taking a major chance."

"We knew there would be cops all over."

"Right. And Josef Smirnoff is dead and bullets were flying everywhere."

She couldn't argue that.

"So, tomorrow, we go back for our checks. Our retainer checks," she murmured.

"And you know we're going to be asked to do something for those checks."

"At least I don't think they're remotely suspicious of us," Jasmine told him.

"Not yet. We're still new."

"Kari came in just ahead of me," Jasmine said. "She…she was a replacement for Mary, I think."

"Here's the thing—what do we do when they want something from us that we don't want to do?" Jorge asked. "We haven't gotten anyone to admit to any criminal activity. If they ask you to be an escort, that's actually legal. So, you go off with someone they set you up with—and that guy wants sex. What do you do? Arrest the guy? That won't get us anywhere. And you sure as hell aren't going to compromise yourself."

"You may be asked first."

"I'm pretty—but not as pretty as you are."

Jasmine laughed. "Beauty is in the eye of the beholder, you know."

"Trust me on this. You'll be first. They'll tread a little more lightly with me."

Jasmine shook her head. "We have to get in more tightly, hear things and find something on them. You're right. They'll deny they have anything to do with illegally selling sex—I'm sure they've got that all worked out." She sighed. "I guess that our FBI connection will do a better job—he'll find out what they're doing with the money."

"How do we prove murder?" Jorge asked softly.

Jasmine lowered her head.

Jorge took her shoulders and spun her around to look at him. "We don't know that Mary is dead."

"I know," she whispered.

She was startled when her phone started to ring; it was a pay-as-you-go phone, one purchased in her cover name, Jasmine Alamein.

She looked at Jorge. "It's Natasha."

"Answer it!"

"Ah, Jasmine, my darling," Natasha said. "I'm so glad to reach you so quickly."

"Yeah, no problem," Jasmine said.

"We have a favor to ask of you. It includes a bonus, naturally."

"What is it?" Jasmine asked. Jorge was staring at her, wary.

"That friend of Josef's—Mr. Marensky. He is new in town. He has asked if you would be so good as to show him around. We'd be happy if you could do so—he came to us, instead of trying to twist our arm for a phone number. You will take him around town, yes? I said that wrong. He wishes to take you to dinner and perhaps you could show him some of the beach. And report to me, of course."

"Yes, for sure. Where do you want me to be when?" Jasmine asked.

"He will call for you at your apartment. Please, make sure your friend is not there when he arrives."

"What time?"

"Eight o'clock tonight."

"Thank you, Natasha. I will be ready."

"Wear something very pretty." Natasha didn't mean pretty. She meant *sexy*.

"I will. Thank you. Thank you!"

"My pleasure. Tomorrow morning you will come back in here."

"Yes, Natasha." Jasmine hung up. Jorge was staring at her. "My first date."

"I was afraid of this."

"She doesn't want you hanging around when my date comes for me."

"Like hell!"

"It's Jacob—*Marensky*."

"Oh." Jorge breathed a sigh of relief.

"I'm just a little worried," Jasmine said.

"About Jacob?"

Jasmine laughed. "Not on that account—I'm not sure he's particularly fond of me."

"You were acting badly."

"I was not—"

"You were."

"Never mind. I'm just wondering what good it's going to do if we just wind up watching one another."

"Trust me. That man has a plan in mind."

"I hope you're right. I'm so worried."

"Jasmine, we just went undercover. You know as well as I do that often cops and agents have to lead a double life for months to get what they're after. Years."

"This can't take that long," she said softly. She didn't add the rest of what she was thinking.

If it did…they might well end up dead themselves.

Chapter Four

Jacob arrived at Jasmine's apartment at precisely 8:00 p.m. She was ready, dressed in a halter dress and wickedly high heels. The assessment he gave her was coolly objective. And his words were even more so.

"You know how to play the part."

"Hey, I'm just a naive young model willing to let a rich guy take me out for an expensive dinner," she told him.

"Jorge?"

"They told me not to have him here."

"What is he doing tonight?"

"Catching up on his favorite cable show," Jasmine said. "Playing it all low."

"At his studio?"

Jasmine nodded and turned away.

Her captain had gone along with this at her say-so. But the FBI seemed to know way

more than the police. She was certain that
Jacob Wolff knew all about her fake dossier
and Jorge's fake dossier, and she felt woefully
late to the party.

"Hey." To her surprise, he caught her by the
shoulders and spun her around. "This isn't a
jurisdictional pissing match, you know. The
FBI started planning the minute we heard from
Smirnoff. You didn't know because we didn't
inform the cops until it was absolutely neces-
sary they knew we were in town. We had no
idea you were in the middle of an undercover
operation—we've had an eye on these guys for
a while. Smirnoff coming in was the opening
we needed."

He was right; they'd both had separate operations going on. And she'd wanted this case.
She'd talked her captain into it being important. The bodies in the oil drums had proved
she was right. Provided they could link them
back to the Deco Gang.

"I'm sorry," she murmured.

"I worked something like this in New York
not that long ago," he told her. "The Bureau
crew I wound up working with hadn't known
about me. It's always like that. A need-to-know

basis. Fewer people to say things that might get you killed."

"Yes, but now—"

"Now, we're in it together. And now we need to head out. Where would you like to have dinner?"

"Wherever."

He grinned. "I'm supposed to be a very rich guy, you know. Oh, and with the power to push ahead at any given restaurant."

"How rude!"

"Yes, absolutely. But we're playing parts. And we need to play those parts well."

"How have your people gotten to so many restaurants?" Jasmine asked.

"They haven't," he said. "No one will say it, but everyone is afraid of the Deco Gang."

"Ah," Jasmine said. "Well, then, we're in the middle of stone crab season. I say we go for the most popular."

"Sure."

As they left her apartment, he slipped his arm through hers. Jasmine stiffened.

"Play along," he murmured.

"You think they're watching?"

"I think they could be at any given time."

She didn't argue that.

"I didn't bring a car. Taxi or an Uber?" he asked.

"I'm fine walking."

"In those shoes?"

She shrugged. "Not my favorite, but we're going about seven blocks. Over a mile in these? I'd say taxi or Uber!"

They walked past T-shirt shops and other restaurants with tables that spilled out on the sidewalk. It was a beautiful night. Balmy. It had to be in the midseventies. Jasmine could smell the salt on the air, and, over the music that escaped from many an establishment, she could hear the water—or at least she could imagine she heard the waves crashing softly up on the shore. Here where they walked, the sand and water were across busy Collins Avenue; the traffic was almost always bumper-to-bumper. She knew young people often came just to cruise the streets, showing off their souped-up cars.

She didn't get it; never had cared for fancy cars.

People in all styles of dress thronged the sidewalks. Some were decked out to the hilt, planning to visit one of the clubs or see a show. Others were casual, out just to shop or dine in a more casual fashion. While the South Beach neighborhood of Miami Beach was trendy and filled with great deco places, boutiques and more, heading farther north, one crossed Lincoln Road, a pedestrian mall and beyond that, a lot of the more staid grande dame hotels from the heyday era when Al Capone and his mobsters had ruled, and later the fabled Rat Pack had entertained, along with other greats.

The beach was like a chameleon, ready to change for every new decade.

At an old and ever-popular restaurant, known for its stone crabs while in season, they did find they were welcomed by a hostess and discreetly—but far too quickly—shown to a table. Jacob had managed, even with the lines outside wrapping around the building, to get them a private table in a little alcove.

Jacob made a pretense of studying the wine menu. He had known, she was certain, exactly what he wanted from the beginning. He wound up ordering champagne—and club soda, as well. She knew as the evening progressed, the champagne would disappear into leftover club soda.

The waitress was gone—they had both ordered the stone crab claws—and he leaned toward her, taking her hand from across the table, rubbing his thumb lightly over her flesh.

"You talked to your people?" he asked softly.

She nodded. "This afternoon. The three men in the oil drums...one has been there, they estimate, about three years. One several months... and one maybe two weeks or so."

Jacob smiled lightly, his expression expertly at odds with their conversation. "Do you know who they might be? They'll be testing, checking dental records. But so far, they don't match anyone reported missing down here." He hesitated. "We're a land of promise, but...people take advantage of that. I recently worked a case in New York... Here's the thing, and the cause of half the world's problems. When you have nothing at all, you have nothing to lose. People from war-torn countries might be desperate and can be drawn in and then forced to do just about anything." He was quiet for a minute. "Some wind up in oil drums."

"And some," she said, "just want more and more—like Victor Kozak."

"So it appears."

"What do you mean, so it appears?"

"Kozak became kingpin. But when Josef Smirnoff came in to the Bureau, he didn't know who intended to kill him. He just…he was afraid. He ruled so much, controlled so much, and yet must have felt like an ancient king. Someone wanted his throne."

"Just like an ancient king—who could plan to overthrow him unless they had a right to follow in his line?"

"That's true. But… I can't get over how lovely you look in that dress," he said suddenly.

She saw that the waiter had arrived, bearing a large silver champagne bucket filled with ice and a bottle.

"You clean up all right yourself," she said softly. And he did. He was wearing a casual soft taupe jacket over a tailored white shirt. He was a handsome man, she thought—with a bit of the look of a Renaissance poet, except she was certain that while his appearance was that of a tall lean man, he was composed of wire-tight muscle beneath.

The waiter smiled and poured their drinks, and they acted like a couple happily out on a date.

Jacob leaned closer to her again, smiling as he lifted his glass to her. "Josef Smirnoff admitted to dealing drugs, arms dealing, prostitution and money laundering. He swore up and down that he didn't order murder."

Jasmine lifted her glass with a dazzling smile, as well. "And yet, one of those bodies discovered had been there a very long time."

"So, someone might have been getting rid of people without Josef Smirnoff knowing."

"And how could that happen?"

"I don't know. We weren't able to get to Smirnoff for more conversation before he was killed. This had all just sprung into being, you know. It's been a complicated case for us. Smirnoff managed to get hold of an agent in the Miami office, but they didn't have anyone down here that they were certain couldn't be compromised—wouldn't be known by anyone. They appealed to the head offices in Virginia. From there, they called on me. I spent a week immersed in everything related to the Deco Gang, and we were lucky that we could arrange paperwork so it appears that I—as Jacob Marensky—own the Dolphin Galleries."

"So, you didn't know Josef Smirnoff?"

"I can't say that I knew him. But I know what he told people. And he was set up with the US Marshals' office—he would have disappeared into witness protection as soon as we had finished our investigation."

Their dinner was arriving.

"Do you really like stone crabs?" she asked him, hoping that her smile was flirtatious. "They're more of a local delicacy. And here's the thing—the crab lives! They take the claw and toss the crab back in. The claw regrows. That's why they're seasonal."

He lowered his head. His smile was legitimate. "Yes, I've had them, and I actually like them very much."

"Can I get you anything else?" their waiter asked. They had their crackers, mustard sauces and drawn butter.

"I think we're just fine," Jacob said.

"Lovely," Jasmine agreed.

The waiter left them.

"So, you think someone other than Victor Kozak arranged the murder? You know that the press—and half the people in the country—think he was caught in another act of random violence."

He nodded. "And we have nothing to say."

Jasmine cracked a claw. A piece of shell went flying across the table, hitting Jacob on the left cheek.

"Oh! Sorry!" she said, somewhat mortified. He laughed. "Not a problem."

"These really aren't date food," Jasmine said. "But then again, we aren't really on a date." She frowned, then made a show of dabbing at his face and laughing. "So, if not Victor Kozak, who would have the power to pull off such a thing as the murder of Josef Smirnoff?"

"It might have been Kozak. If not, there's Ivan Petrov, bartender and manager."

"You think he's high enough on the food chain?"

"Depends on who is in on the coup."

"The only people as close to management as Ivan are the bodyguards—I like to think of them as the Three Stooges."

"On steroids," Jacob said.

"Yes, deadly Stooges," she agreed.

"So, Victor Kozak, Ivan Petrov, Natasha Volkov—and the Stooges," he said.

"I just wonder about the bodyguards. The others are all Russian or Ukrainian, but Alejandro is Colombian, and Antonio is Italian."

"Half Italian," Jacob told her. "His mother is English."

"You do know more than I do."

"They are equal-opportunity crooks," Jacob

said drily. "Any group down here can find power elsewhere—even elsewhere around the country."

"Their bookkeeper is from Atlanta," Jasmine murmured.

"Good old Southern boy."

"Girl."

"Pardon?"

"Good old Southern girl," Jasmine said. "And yet..."

"Yet?"

"I don't think she really knows about the criminal enterprises. She gets money after it's been laundered. As far as paperwork goes, they're enterprising citizens, paying their taxes."

"Well, Ivan is deep into it all," Jacob told her. "He was waiting at the gallery when I went in this morning. We made arrangements for the sale of one of the paintings in the gallery."

"As a way to move money?"

"Yeah. He paid way more than the painting is worth. The funds will go into an offshore account. It's all setup."

"So they believe in you?"

"For now..."

He had been studiously cracking a shell.

This time, his piece of shell flew across the table—catching Jasmine right in the cleavage.

"Sorry!"

She caught the shell quickly before he could. But the gentleman in him came through; he started to move but stopped. The two of them laughed together. Honest laughter, and it was nice.

"Not really date food," he said. "Unless I were more accomplished at this, of course."

"I don't think you could be much more accomplished," she muttered, afraid that a bit of envy and maybe even bitterness might have made it through in her voice. She caught his curious look. "You speak half a dozen languages," she explained.

He shrugged. "I was just lucky. My family— much like yours—is a mini United Nations. Everyone from everywhere. And I love language. It gets easier to pick up another, if you know the Romance languages, the Latin base always helps for reading, even if it takes a bit. But all languages have rules—well, except for English! It's the hardest. Luckily, it was my first."

"Still…it's impressive."

"You speak Spanish."

"Picked up from growing up in South Florida. Half of my friends are Cuban, Colombian or from somewhere in the islands or South America."

"Or Brazil."

"I do also know a bit of Portuguese," she agreed.

They both smiled again. "So…we're equal-opportunity law enforcement, dealing with equal-opportunity criminals," Jasmine mused.

"So we are," he said. "Let's wander on down Washington Street. We'll stop and have dessert and coffee somewhere else."

"You think we're being followed?"

"I think we're definitely being watched in one way or another."

He paid the check and they left.

"You're from here, right?" he asked her.

"You know all about me, right?" she returned, looking at him.

"Well, I do now. I swear, when I tackled you… I didn't."

"You knew there were cops on the scene."

"They didn't tell me that one of the cops was a woman—modeling as if she were accustomed to the runway. But then you are, correct?"

"You received a full dossier on me after the

fact?" Jasmine asked. "I wish that the powers that be might have returned the favor."

"I'm an open book," he told her.

"I'll bet."

"I knew from the time I was a kid I wanted to be in the FBI," Jacob told her. "I had a great uncle who was gunned down—for having the same name as a criminal. He was killed by mistake. Anyway, I got into a military academy, served time in the army and immediately joined the FBI. I've done a lot of undercover work. I seem to blend in well with an accepted and ambiguous foreign criminal look."

"Or latent hippie," she told him.

He grinned.

"If you want to see some of South Florida, I can show you around," she told him.

He smiled, lowering his head. "Great. I grew up here. But you know South Florida better than I do."

She grinned. "I was born here."

"Oh?"

"We traveled a lot—but always lived here. Well, not *here*, but in Miami, in Coconut Grove."

"There are so many areas… An amazing city, really. I think, just four decades or so ago, the population of the area was about three hundred thousand. Now, we're looking at millions." He cast a grimace her way. "Populations always lead to crime," he added.

He could be incredibly mercurial. He slipped an arm around her shoulder and pointed to a café before them. "They're known for their crème brûlée. Shall we?"

"Crème brûlée," she agreed, frowning slightly.

He lowered his head close to hers. "We are being followed," he said, pretending to nuzzle her forehead. "Ten o'clock, just down the street. Our dear friend Alejandro Suarez."

She was careful not to look right away, but let out a tone of delighted laughter and planted a kiss on his cheek.

"Let's have dessert," she said louder.

He took her arm and led her into the café.

"Well," she said as they sat close together. "I'm not sure if we've gotten anywhere, but the stone crab claws were delicious, and this is wonderful crème brûlée."

"Definitely better than some of the undercover work I've done before," he told her. He made a face. "Homeless detail. Sleeping in boxes—and for dinner, French fries out of the garbage."

"Yuck."

"You do what's called for."

"I would have...for this," she murmured.

"So, tell me about Mary. Tell me why you're on this case."

She stared up at him, startled. Somehow, he seemed to know everything. She hesitated and then shrugged.

"Our watchdog has stayed outside," he said softly.

She nodded. He was good at observation; she trusted him.

"Mary," she began. "The Deco Gang has been on our radar for a long time—they've operated out of restaurants, bars and even dry cleaners, moving on all the time. My usual cases keep me on the mainland. MDPD comes in on cases in many of the cities—Miami-Dade County is made up of thirty-four cities now, with more incorporating all the time. Not all the smaller cities have their own major crime divisions, and so we handle a great deal of it. South Beach does have a major crime unit, but the powers that be approved of us taking over this case. Miami Beach cops had a greater risk of being recognized, even undercover. It's not that they tried to hand off work—it was just a better plan. And honestly, until the bodies were found… I might have been the detective taking it the most seriously. Jurisdiction on this is complicated. The oil drums you saw were discovered up in Broward County, by a Seminole law enforcement official."

"There's the Florida Department of Law Enforcement. They could have taken over."

"And those guys are great. But going in on this, it fell to something Miami-Dade would do. We were investigating a disappearance. We were suspicious of the Deco Gang. And when it came to finding a way to slip in and be close enough, the models the clubs use all the time seemed a good cover. I approached my captain about it."

"You were in."

She shrugged. "In all honesty, I was afraid if I mentioned that a friend of mine had been working with the gang's models and then disappeared, it would be a strike against me in terms of being able to take the case. But it actually worked in my favor—I really knew her, I could talk about her and maybe get some information from the other young women working with them. And Mary, well, she's one of the nicest people you'd ever hope to meet. She looks for the good in everyone. Since I'm a cop, she thinks I'm jaded—though I actually think I'm pretty nice, too. Cops don't have to be asses."

"No, they don't," Jacob agreed, clearly somewhat amused.

"But Mary's problem is that she does look for the good. She has to be slapped in the face by bad to see that it exists."

"She probably is a very good person."

"Kari Anderson—the girl on the runway with me when Josef was shot—reminds me of Mary. They're both natural blondes with huge blue eyes and a trusting manner to go with them. Mary was working dinner theater, but not making much money. She saw the ad for models. She did a few shows with the group—Smirnoff's group is behind a number of entertainment offerings. They've been doing legitimate business, too. They own a bunch of other nightclubs. Anyway, Mary got swept up with Natasha and Josef and what she was doing…and saw no evil in it. And she was excited to get paid so well. Florida is a right-to-work state, so dinner theater may be a group requiring Actors' Equity, but then again, it may not be. She was thrilled. She paid her rent two months ahead with her paycheck from one show. And then there was the regular retainer just for being at the clubs, filling them with beautiful young people… It was easy money at first."

"Did she say anything to you about being nervous?"

Jasmine shook her head. "Never." She hesitated. "The last time I talked to Mary, she was excited. She was going to be a star attraction, working their next show. Which was the opening of the club the other night."

"The one you starred in instead."

"Yes. Look, Mary never said anything to me. She wasn't nervous, as far as I know. She just disappeared. A few weeks ago, she was supposed to meet me for lunch. She didn't show up. Mary's parents passed away when she was eighteen. She's on her own, an only child. She and I have been friends forever—we went all the way through grade school and high school together. We have other friends, but no one else has any other information about her. I don't even know how long she's actually been missing. After she missed our date, I called and called. We had an officer from Missing Persons go in to talk to Josef and Natasha, and they both appeared mystified—according to the officer."

"Have you gotten anything?"

"Not yet. The girls are still getting to know me. No one expected what happened to Josef. But apparently, we're all on retainer. Including Jorge."

"Retainer," Jacob murmured.

"I'm not sure what's next. Jorge and I can go in for checks tomorrow."

"Good. I'll stop by at some point." Jacob leaned back. "Well, I believe I'm supposed to walk you back now."

She nodded, oddly sorry that the evening was ending. It was work. Dangerous work.

Work to find Mary.

"You think we're still being watched?" she asked.

"I do."

He paid, stood and drew out her chair. He very politely took her arm and opened the door for her as they exited the café. He slipped an arm around her shoulders.

"Alejandro still around?" Jasmine asked.

"I think he was sitting at one of the outside tables…that's the back of his head behind us. Nope, he's rising now. I'd say he's going to make sure that I take you home and then leave—not overstepping my bounds."

They walked at a lazy pace, his arm around her but with all propriety.

"Interesting," she murmured.

"What's that?"

"How I'm going to discover that they keep control. I mean, as far as they know, I'm just a girl trying to get ahead in modeling. What if I just liked you and wanted to be with you?"

"I don't know. But if I went outside the rules…"

"I'm wondering if we'd both wind up in oil drums. I can see how they'd blame you. You're officially on the inside. But—"

"You're just an innocent. Well, in their eyes."

They'd reached her apartment. She was in a charming place, ground floor, almost in front of the pool. He walked her to the door and then paused. She wound up with her back against the wall by her door. He had a hand on the wall and was leaning against her.

He lowered his face toward hers and gave her a slow careful kiss. She allowed a hand to fall on his chest, and she wished that she didn't feel that there was absolutely nothing wrong with him. His scent was clean and masculine, mixed with the salty cool ocean air. His chest was vital and alive and yet like a rock. His lips were…

He drew away from her.

"I think that was just right. You might want to smile and laugh and then go in."

"Alejandro is watching?"

"He's right out on the street."

"Lovely, what a lovely night," she said, letting her voice carry.

"I'm sure we'll see each other again," Jacob said. "If you're willing…"

"I just have to check my work schedule."

"Of course." He stepped back, and she turned and let herself into her apartment.

She swung the door shut and slid the locks. And then, she stood there for a long, long time. She brought her fingers to her lips. They felt as if they were on fire.

Chapter Five

"You will pay Mr. Chavez twenty-five thousand for the painting," Victor Kozak told Jacob.

They were seated in the office at the rear of the gallery Jacob was pretending to own. Jacob nodded sagely to Kozak. They had already been through the niceties. They both sat with little demitasse cups of espresso. Kozak had admired the shop. Jacob had expressed his appreciation for Kozak's patronage.

"I don't know this artist," Jacob said.

"Trust me. He is excellent."

"And my commission?"

"Fifteen percent."

Jacob let that sit. He smiled at Kozak. "No disrespect. Twenty percent." He was pretty sure that in all such haggling—legal and illegal—Kozak had a higher limit than the figure he'd started with.

"Eighteen," Kozak said.

"I'm looking forward to working with you. Seeing that wonderful art arrives in our country. But if we're to go forward in the future, I believe we need a set rate now. I will be an excellent gallery to procure all the right artists—but I need to survive. The overhead here is quite high," Jacob told him.

Kozak was thoughtful. "All right, then. Twenty percent."

He rose; their dealings were complete. Jacob stood as well and the two men shook hands.

"Have the police come up with anything as yet regarding the shooter? Or shooters?" Jacob asked.

"No, nothing they have shared. You said *shooters*. You think that more than one man was involved?"

"We both know guns," Jacob told Kozak. "Yes, the shots were coming from at least two angles, maybe three."

"Accomplices," Kozak said, shaking his head. "So much violence in this world." He sighed as he lowered his head in sorrow. "Josef was a good man." He shrugged, a half smile on his face. "A good man—for all that we are.

He was simply a businessman, and he had integrity in what he did."

Drugs and prostitution, if not murder. But sometimes, even criminals had their ethics.

"All the security," Jacob said, "and still—"

"Don't worry. What the police don't discover, we will," Kozak assured him.

"Naturally," Jacob said.

"I'm so sorry that this happened. Josef… was your friend?"

"We had a few business deals years ago. Art, you know, is always in the eye of the beholder. He'd commissioned a few pieces through me in my galleries before. When I wanted to come south—no more chipping ice off windows, you know—I looked down here and saw that Josef was opening a club. It's always prudent to establish relationships before opening a business anywhere," Jacob said.

"Josef told me about you." Kozak smiled. "And we do nothing without checking out references. I know that Josef trusted you. But now…his body will be released on Friday, they tell me."

"And there will be a funeral?"

"Yes, it will be at a little Russian Orthodox

church in the city, not on the beach. A private affair. But you will be invited."

"I appreciate the honor and privilege of saying goodbye to an old friend," Jacob told him. "And with your permission, I will be by this afternoon with a small token for our new friendship."

"That will be fine. The club will reopen Friday night, but invitation only. A very small group to begin. We must show the world that we're now a safe place to be."

"This violence... It can happen anywhere. Lightning doesn't usually strike the same place twice. I believe the club will be fine."

Kozak gave him a rueful grin. "Sometimes, such events make a place a curiosity. Think back to the '80s. Paul Castellano and Thomas Bilotti were gunned down in a hit ordered by Gotti in front of Sparks Steak House in New York. The restaurant is still going strong. Down here, Al Capone was often in a suite at the Biltmore Hotel in Coral Gables. The suite is very expensive, and people still love to take it—even though Thomas 'Fatty' Walsh was gunned down at the hotel, supposedly over a gambling dispute." His smile deepened. "The hotel did go down after hurricanes and the Depression. It became a veteran's hospital. It was empty—and very haunted—but it's back to being very chic today."

"Let's hope we don't all have to go down first."

"Not to worry about us. Josef created a strong group of business associates. We will be fine." With that, Kozak took his leave.

Jacob walked him to the door. They both smiled at Jacob's "assistant," who was busy behind the old art nouveau desk that served as their register and counter. Katrina smiled back and waved.

She was a perfect choice for this role. Katrina Partridge had been with the Bureau for nearly twenty years. She was in her midforties, attractive and able to carry off both charm and a completely businesslike demeanor. She also knew the art world backward and forward.

When Jacob was gone, she shook her head, indicating they shouldn't talk in the gallery. She pointed to his office, and he followed her there.

"He was walking around a long time. I think he touched a few of the frames, and… I could be wrong. But he could have planted some kind of a bug."

"Good observation, thank you. So, we're being given our first commission," he told her.

"But that's not enough," Katrina said.

"We could bring him down," Jacob told her. "But there will be a work of art, and who is to say what a work of art is worth?"

"Someone who knows art," she said drily.

"But art is subjective."

"So true. Yes, you're right."

"We're after killers," he said softly. "That's what we want to nail them on."

"I know," Katrina said. "And hey, what's not to like about this assignment? I don't have much going on yet—I'm enjoying my downtime. Sand, beach, lovely weather…"

"Still, be careful, Katrina. We can never know when something may slip. They gunned down a man in a room full of cops and security."

"I'm always careful," she said. She smiled, indicating her back.

She was dressed in a fashionable skirt and blouse ensemble with a handsome tailored jacket. Despite the tailoring, he could see—

when she indicated her back—that she was not without her Glock.

He smiled his acknowledgment but found himself worrying about Jasmine Adair.

Modeling. There was no hiding a weapon when dressers were around, making sure that a gown was being worn properly. And she was into it on a personal level—something that was dangerous from the get-go.

He had no right to interfere; her operation had begun before his and they were now required to work together. He had no problem working with police.

It was just that he was attracted to her. He didn't think it possible not to be. She was unique; elegant and a bit reserved, and yet when she smiled, when she laughed, she was warm, vibrant and sensual.

He turned his mind from thoughts of her.

"I'll bring the caviar over in about an hour," he told Katrina.

"All ready, in the container in back. I've dressed it up beautifully, if I do say so myself."

"I'm sure you did," he told her.

They moved back into the gallery. Jacob made a point of informing her that they were commissioning a piece, one that had a buyer already, who was in love with the artist's work.

She made mention of a local up-and-coming artist the buyer might like, as well.

A real customer sauntered into the room. Jacob returned to his office but found himself sitting and doing nothing but thinking.

He had to find a way in that was tighter; he had to be close to Jasmine.

He was still wary, of course. She hadn't turned him into a fool.

Maybe she had. Jacob hadn't felt such an instant attraction…almost a longing…in years.

Not since Sabrina.

"Ah, you are so beautiful, even in mourning," Natasha told Jasmine, admiring the way the draped black dress fell in sweeps to the floor. "Remember, at this, you will be quiet. You will help our guests with their drinks and food but keep a distance. Victor has ordered that this be a solemn occasion. You understand?"

"Yes, Natasha," Jasmine assured her.

Natasha looked over at Jorge, handsome in a conservative black suit. "You two will do well, I believe." She called to the little seamstress who hurried over. "I don't think that the hem needs to come up, but at the waist…a half an inch?"

"Yes, ma'am, of course," the seamstress said. She poked and prodded at Jasmine for a minute, pinning the waist and then nodding.

Jasmine thanked her. The tiny woman helped her slip out of the dress, and carried it away.

As Jasmine reached for her jeans and T-shirt, she was aware that Natasha was assessing her again—as she might assess meat in a market.

"So, last night, you were charming?"

"Yes, he took me for a nice dinner, and I told him about the beach."

"Very good. He likes you."

"I believe so."

Natasha turned away. "You could be asked to do much worse," she said, almost to herself, rather than to Jasmine. "So, now…jeans and a T-shirt. You must dress more…ah, how do I say this? Much prettier, to come in here."

"Business clothes."

"No, the halter dress you wore last night. Very pretty. And heels. No sneakers."

"Definitely, whatever you say."

"Victor would like to see you. I wish there was more time…time for you to go home. Ah, what am I thinking? I still have clothing from the show!" Natasha beamed, and caught Jasmine's hand. "No, no. Don't put your jeans back on."

"Oh…okay."

Natasha left her standing on the little podium where dresses were fitted and headed back to the racks of clothing that remained hanging in the massive closet space. She searched through the racks until she evidently found something that pleased her.

When she returned, she had hangers that bore a sleeveless silk blouse and a red skirt. "These will do," she said.

The skirt was short. Very short.

Jasmine donned the clothing. She smiled, hoping to show that she was feeling friendly with Natasha. "I don't think that the sneakers go with this so well."

"Ah, but of course not! You're an eight and a half, American size, in shoes?"

"Nine," Jasmine told her.

A very large shoe size, apparently, in Natasha's opinion. "Ah, well, you are tall."

She was five-ten. Natasha would be appalled by Jasmine's mom—just five-eight and she wore an eleven.

Natasha brought shoes—four-inch stilettos. "These will be beautiful," she said.

Jasmine slipped on the shoes. She was well over six-feet, now.

"So, come. Victor is happy with you." She turned to Jorge. "You—you will come on Friday evening. The service is at two. Josef will be interred after, and then we will be arriving here."

"Yes, ma'am," Jorge said.

Natasha studied him for a minute and then smiled. "We may have more work for you soon. Showing people Miami Beach—and all its pleasures."

Jasmine knew Jorge well. He didn't miss a beat. "Thank you," he said.

"And, now, you..." Natasha took Jasmine's hand. "Come and see Victor."

"For sure, a pleasure," Jasmine said.

"I'll wait here," Jorge said cheerfully.

"No, Jorge, you are done for today. Antonio will see you out."

Antonio was standing at the door to the large dressing room.

"Call you later!" Jasmine told him cheerfully.

She wasn't feeling so cheerful; she was

caught here with nothing, no backup—and she was off to see Victor. She wasn't worried for her life. If she was going to be taken out, they'd have gone after Jorge, too.

Had she done too well with Jacob "Marensky"? Was she now going to be asked to entertain another of their associates?

There was really no choice but to play it out. She had to wonder if this was where Mary had stood—right before she had disappeared.

With a smile, Jasmine watched Jorge go—and she accompanied Natasha to Victor Kozak's office.

Victor Kozak was not alone.

There was a man in his office. A tall man, he wore a designer suit in charcoal gray. He was perhaps in his midfifties, with iron-gray hair and mustache and watery blue eyes.

They'd both been sitting; Victor behind the desk, the new man in one of the upholstered chairs set before it. They stood politely.

"Ah, Jasmine. I'd like you to meet Mr. Connor," Victor said. "He's visiting from England and knows nothing about Miami Beach. He's hoping you will show him the beach, and to the finest hotel."

JACOB WAS ALREADY on his way to the club when his phone rang. He glanced at the number; he hadn't saved any in his contacts, but rather memorized the last four digits of those he needed to know.

Jorge Fuentes was calling.

"Where are you?" Jorge asked.

"Heading to the club. Why?"

"Head faster. I think they've taken Jasmine in to entertain a client. I mean, she can handle herself, but this is happening way too fast."

"Picking up the pace," Jacob moved forward quickly. "I'll be back in touch as soon as possible."

He didn't run; he might have been observed. But he could walk fast as hell and he did so. He came to the corner of Washington Street and rounded it, heading to the employee side entrance to the club.

This time, Antonio was leaning against the wall by the door, smoking a cigarette, watching the day.

"Those things will kill you," Jacob said.

"Mr. Marensky. I don't believe we were expecting you."

"I have something for Mr. Kozak. He was

just in the shop, you know. I need to get right up there."

Jacob didn't wait for Antonio to respond but hurried past him in a way that meant the goon's only action could be to physically accost him, and the man would still be trying to figure out if Jacob was important enough or not to get through.

Suarez was in the hall.

Jacob made a point of striding past him with a huge grin on his face. "Present for Victor!" he declared, lifting the ice chest filled with caviar that Katrina had so beautifully decorated with multicolored ribbons.

He burst into the office before he could be stopped.

Kozak immediately stood, reaching toward his jacket—and the weapon he surely carried there, Jacob thought. But he didn't draw the weapon.

Good. Jacob was trusted.

Jasmine was there, outfitted like the very expensive and exclusive call girl she was apparently expected to be.

A man had just been leaning over her—either inspecting her or seeking a better look at her cleavage. He was tall and solid, though his face was lined—perhaps from years of worriedly looking over his shoulder. His eyes were a strange, cool blue. Like ice.

"Victor! A present. Forgive me for interrupting. My source delivered this just this morning, and after we spoke—" He paused. "Excuse me, sir. No disrespect intended. I was in a rush—Jasmine!" he said, breaking up his own run of words. "Hello, and thank you again for last evening. You were a wonderful tour guide."

"I was conducting business with Mr. Connor—" Kozak began.

Jacob brought a frown to his face, and then allowed himself to appear deeply disturbed. "No, sir," he said, addressing Connor.

Connor straightened and stared at Kozak. "Kozak, I want—"

"I'm afraid I already have an interest," Jacob said softly.

"She's just a woman," Kozak muttered beneath his breath.

Jacob was glad that Jasmine appeared not to have heard the words. "Forgive me, but, Mr. Kozak, you're a very busy man. This arrangement was made. Yesterday. And at the show, before he was killed, I received promises from Josef Smirnoff."

"Smirnoff is dead," Connor said.

"But not forgotten," Jacob said.

Kozak was, of course, in a tight position. If he hadn't murdered Josef Smirnoff and was taking over as a natural progression, he had to respect promises made by his predecessor.

"Not forgotten, no. And honored," Kozak murmured. Jacob had given him an out—and he was glad to see that the man wanted his "business" and was willing to take the out.

Jacob turned to Connor.

"I'm new, but… I understand this. Miss Alamein and I had dinner last night and arranged for a sightseeing tour this evening. I had forgotten to tell Mr. Kozak about my tickets, but I'm afraid that I did specify this…young woman."

"I can make even better arrangements for you, Mr. Connor," Kozak said. "You must understand, we are in mourning right now. And in honor of Josef, I must follow through on all his promises."

"Fine. Call me when you have found a suitable companion," Connor told Kozak. He was looking at Jacob. Sizing him up. Apparently, he determined that the companionship of a certain woman was not worth a battle. He turned and left without another word.

"So, before you came to me... Josef had promised you this woman," Kozak said.

Jacob didn't look at Jasmine. Knowing her as he was coming to know her, he was amazed that she was managing to just sit still.

"When I saw her on the runway," he said, his voice husky, "I knew I wanted her at that moment. I believe she might have been his last promise."

"Then I will make no other arrangements. But you must remember, Miss Alamein is in my employ. And she will appear when she is needed."

"That is understood."

Kozak walked over to Jasmine. "You will honor this arrangement?" he asked her.

Jasmine stood. In the heels she was wearing, she was eye level with Kozak. She smiled sweetly. "As you wish, Mr. Kozak."

"Fine," Kozak said. "Just remember, you work for me," he added softly.

"Always," she told him earnestly. Jasmine's smile deepened. "And thank you, sir. Thank you. Mr. Marensky and I were able to have the most delicious dinner last night. Far more easily than I might have ever imagined!"

Even Kozak seemed caught by her charm. "My pleasure. So, I believe that Natasha wanted to talk with you one more time. And…" he gave his attention back to Jacob "…Miss Alamein will be ready for you tonight, for these tickets you have."

"I'll wait and escort her home now," Jacob said. "Sir, if you have a minute, the present I brought… I believe you will enjoy it immensely. It is Almas, from the beluga sturgeon—supposed to be some of the finest caviar. I must admit, I am not an expert, but I have been assured by those who are that this is delicious."

"Then you must sit and enjoy it with me," Kozak said. He waved a hand at Jasmine. "See Natasha, see what she needs from you."

Jasmine was dismissed. She left the room.

Jacob looked at Kozak. "I thank you for respecting me—and Josef's memory," he said. "And I would like to do more."

"Oh?"

"I am not without certain skills. I would like your permission to look into Josef's death myself."

BREATHING WAS DIFFICULT.

Jasmine's heart was pounding. She'd been so sure of herself, even in Kozak's office with the very strange *Mr.* Connor all but pawing her, that she'd been figuring out ways to handle the situation herself. Alone with the man, she'd have figured out something…

And blown her cover. And all hope of finding out what had happened to Mary.

She hurried down the hall—smiling at Sasha, on duty there now—to the dressing room. Natasha was at one of the tables, studying her face in the mirror.

She looked at Jasmine, and as she did so, Jasmine had to wonder if the woman's eyes could stretch out of her head, or if she had ears that could extend down a hallway.

Natasha already knew what had happened.

"It's not good," she said. "It's not good at all. One man should not become so possessive."

Jasmine shrugged. "Does it matter?" she asked. "Does it matter if the money is the same?"

"Ah, child, you're new to this," Natasha said.

"Yes, I am. And I am ignorant but willing to learn."

Natasha seemed pleased with her reply. "He

will start to think that he owns you and that he would be better off just spiriting you away somewhere. You must be careful and declare your loyalty to us at all times, do you understand?"

"Yes, Natasha. And I am loyal, I promise you."

"And," Natasha added, "you like this Jacob Marensky?"

"He's clean and he smells good. And he is younger."

Natasha waved a hand in the air. "Yes, he is clean and young and smells good. And young can be good. Old men, with their hopes and their prayers and their pills… They have no idea how often those they think they control sit there and do nothing but laugh at their faulty efforts." She shook her head; Jasmine had the feeling she had experienced the worst and earned her way out of it.

"So then, you may have your jeans and your T-shirt. Apparently, Mr. Marensky is a more casual man and you are going on a sightseeing tour." She shuddered as if a sightseeing tour might be akin to torture.

"Thank you," Jasmine said. "I must admit, the shoes…the heels are a lot."

"They make you very tall. Then again, Mr. Marensky is very tall." She waved a hand in the air. "Josef admired the man. Victor believes that he is an admirable man as well, who understands our business but demands that we respect his. You will, of course, report to me."

"Yes, I will."

Jasmine heard voices. A few of the other girls had arrived.

Kari Anderson came into the room, carrying a bundle of clothes. Behind her were Jen Talbot, Renee Dumas and Helen Lee. They were like a palette of beauty—Kari so pale, Jen olive-skinned, Renee almost ebony and Helen extraordinary with her mix of Eurasian features and lustrous long black hair. They were beautiful on a runway.

They had also been hired to please all tastes.

Thus far, though, she hadn't seen any of the women forced into anything. Just pretty girls with an understanding that they could be paid well for their company. She had sat silently herself as Victor had introduced her to Mr. Connor and informed her that he needed a guide and an escort for the evening. What if she had protested?

Had Mary protested?

"I'll just grab my things and change and get out of here," Jasmine said. "And hang these up."

She fled over to the hangers, finding that her clothing had not been hung—just folded as if with distaste and left on the shelving above the racks. She eased out of the shoes and slid out of the skirt.

Kari walked in. "I'm going to need that skirt, I hear," she said.

"Oh?" Jasmine handed her the skirt on its hanger and shimmied the blouse over her head.

"I'm going to go see Mr. Connor," Kari said. She sounded slightly nervous.

"Are you afraid of him?" Jasmine asked in a whisper. "If so—"

"No, no. He's supposed to be very nice."

"I thought he was new."

"No. Mary went out with him. Just dinner. She said he was very nice. Oh, sorry, you didn't know Mary. She was great, but… I guess this wasn't for her. Me, I want the runway. And if it means dating a few losers…" Her voice trailed. "Dating," she repeated drily. "Okay, having sex with a few repulsive specimens… Well, I managed to choose a lot of losers on my own!

Might as well have it be worth something in the end, I guess."

"Kari?" Natasha called.

"Excuse me," Kari said to Jasmine. "I have to run!"

Jasmine caught her hand. "Kari—please. Will you call me tomorrow and let me know that you're all right?"

Kari seemed surprised. "Of course, I'll be all right. But thank you. And I will call you— we can maybe have lunch or something?"

"I'd love to have lunch," Jasmine assured her. She hesitated. "It's allowed?"

"Oh, yes. They like us to be friends. Sometimes…"

"Sometimes?"

"Kari!" Natasha called again.

"Later!" Kari told her, and with a swirl of blond hair, she was gone.

KOZAK HAD OPENED a bottle of his special "very Russian" vodka to go with the caviar. Jacob was careful to pretend to sip as much as the crime tsar but imbibe as little as possible.

His time with the man was proving to be very interesting.

Kozak talked about growing up in Russia—

about the KGB coming for his father in the middle of the night.

"That must have been very hard on a child," Jacob said.

Kozak shrugged. "My father, he was a killer. When it all broke apart, though…everyone was running. The kind of crime was brutal, from all manner of directions. My mother, bless her, got us out. I never understood. Business is business, but…"

He paused and looked hard at Jacob, very sober despite the vodka he had all but inhaled. "You think you can find Josef's killer?"

Jacob weighed his words carefully. "There have been certain…events in my past that required me to take a closer look at them. I have a talent for uncovering things." He paused. "You really have no idea who killed him?"

Kozak frowned.

"No disrespect," Jacob said quickly. "I liked Josef. We did very good business together. But perhaps, something was going on with the group that was dangerous to all."

"You're talking about the bodies discovered in the Everglades," Kozak said. "There is talk of little but that and the shooting on the news these days. We have even ceased to care about politics, eh? When people are scared…"

He paused and shrugged again. "We had nothing to do with those bodies. Not Josef, not me. And I do not know who killed him. Me, I have kept my boys close—Sasha, Antonio and Alejandro. I have played the game, I have become the king. But you are a newcomer. Down here, that is. Josef trusted you. You know how to stand your ground. You tell me—who killed Josef?"

"I don't know, but as I said, with your permission, I will find out."

"You have my permission—and my blessing. What else do you need?"

"Permission to speak with your boys. And Ivan and Natasha. Whether wittingly or not, Victor, one of them helped the killers."

There was a tap at the door.

"It's me, Mr. Kozak," Jasmine said in a small voice.

"I will see her home," Jacob said, rising and heading to the door. "And I will begin tomorrow. I will find the killer, I promise you."

"Then most definitely, the woman is yours—along with my gratitude," Kozak told him.

Jacob nodded and opened the door. And capturing Jasmine's hand, he hurried down the stairs, Jasmine in his wake.

Chapter Six

"I should have gone with him," Jasmine murmured.

The look Jacob gave her could have turned her to stone. She supposed, in his mind, he had managed not only to save her from a fate worse than death—or actual death, for that matter—but to keep up their undercover guises, as well.

"No, no," she amended quickly. "You were wonderful, magnificent. I mean, you pulled that off, and normal circumstances—"

"Just wait. Wait until we reach your apartment," he said. "At this point, I'm pretty sure it's okay if I come in."

"Are we being followed?"

"Maybe. You never know."

She was surprised when he pulled out his phone. He had such a grip on her with his left hand that she could hear the voice of the man he was calling from his phone in his right hand.

"You got her out?" the voice asked.

Jorge.

"Yes." Jacob glanced her way. "I need tickets, fast. Some kind of sightseeing trip. First available."

"Call you right back."

"Tickets?" Jasmine murmured.

"Tickets."

They were almost to her apartment when the phone rang again. This time, Jorge was speaking more softly.

"Lincoln Road Mall," Jacob relayed.

"We can walk it," Jasmine suggested.

"Then keep walking."

He was angry; she hadn't had a chance to explain yet what she'd meant about wishing she'd gone with Mr. Connor. And on the street the way they were, unaware of how things might go, despite the stand Jacob had just made, he clearly didn't want her talking.

His pace was urgent; she had long legs, and she could trek it, but he was moving fast. They were some distance from the club on Washington Street when he finally seemed to slow—perhaps having burned off some of his energy.

She managed to retrieve her hand from his hold and slide an arm through his, drawing herself close and speaking softly, as if she whispered a lover's words.

"I may have found out how Mary disappeared—and with whom," she told him.

He turned and frowned at her.

"I finally got a second with Kari. She's probably going to wind up going off with this man, Connor. Jacob, Mary met with Connor. She met him—and then she disappeared."

"And you were willing to take that kind of a chance?"

Jasmine swallowed, leaning on his shoulder. "That's what I'm here for. But I didn't find out until after you came and got me out of the room. I saw Kari when I went back to get my own clothing. That's when she told me…and they're going to send her in to be his escort. Jacob, we have to find a way to follow that man. Maybe Jorge—"

"No, Jorge still has an in. And they'd wonder what he was doing. Let me call my office. They'll get someone on it."

He pulled out his phone again. They'd reached Lincoln Road Mall—a pedestrian walkway that offered dozens of shops and restaurants, fun places to dine and enjoy a coffee, a drink, entertainment or an evening.

"It's a private tour company," Jacob said, pointing to a spot by the theaters on Alton Road. "They'll pick us up there."

He veered in that direction, speaking quickly to someone on the phone and giving them the information they had on Connor. Jacob described him to a T. But Jasmine knew he had little else to go on.

She heard rapid questions in return, and then assurances.

"I believe that's ours," Jacob said, pointing to a limo with a sunroof.

The vehicle made a U-turn and pulled to the corner. The driver, a young man in a suit, hopped out and offered them a broad professional smile. "Marensky?" he asked.

"Yes, thank you, Jasmine and Jacob," Jacob said, sliding his phone back into his pocket.

"I'm David Hernandez, your guide for the day!" he said cheerfully. "I'm at your disposal. Now, I understand you're new to the beach, so I'll give you a few suggestions. My first pick is the Ancient Spanish Monastery, but that's north on the beach, so…"

"That's fine," Jacob said quickly. "Is that

okay, honey?" he asked Jasmine, and then he told their guide, "Jasmine knows the place. Me, I'm new."

"I love the Spanish Monastery!" she said. "But I'm not sure I'd be the best guide."

David looked at his watch. "Well, if we move, you can have a couple of hours there. Your assistant ordered a driver and guide until midnight, so—"

"We'll start with the Spanish Monastery," Jacob said.

They slid into the car. With the beach traffic, it was going to take them a few minutes to reach what Jasmine considered to be one of their most intriguing destinations.

"I grew up here, but not on the beach," Jasmine told David.

"Cool. I grew up in the city, by the old Flagler Dog Track—Magic City Casino now," David told them. "People say Miami is young, no history. But we've got tons of it. I could go on forever. But—"

"Please, do, go on forever," Jacob said.

He leaned back in the plush seat of the limo, closing his eyes for a minute. It was the only indication Jasmine had seen that his world could cause him pressure.

He had come in, guns blazing, for her.

She leaned back, as well. She really needed to talk to Captain Lorenzo and give her report. Lorenzo could get cops out after Kari and Connor.

"Of course, South Beach itself is a tourist attraction," David said. "Did you know that it was the original area that was populated? Believe it or not, the beach started out as farmland. The City of Miami itself incorporated on July 28, 1896. Julia Tuttle, our founding mom, had sent an orange blossom to Henry Flagler, convincing him to bring his railroad down— we were almost always frost free!

"The City of Miami Beach was incorporated on March 26, 1915. Now, Miami Beach is comprised of natural and man-made barrier islands. In 1870, Henry and Charles Lum— father and son, by the way, bought a lot of the bracken, sandy, nothing land that's worth billions today. There was a station to help shipwreck victims up north of where you're staying, closer to where we'll be today. They started off with a coconut plantation, but that didn't go so well. Enter some rich Yankees, and the beach started developing.

"Collins Avenue is so named because of an

entrepreneur called Collins. He mixed up the crops and got things going. Then with Miami up and running, the railroad coming down and Government Cut created, people were on their way to thinking it would make a great resort area. Enter the Lummus family, who were bankers, and Carl C. Fisher from Indianapolis, who worked with the Collins and Pancoast group, and by the beginning of the twentieth century, Miami Beach was on its way."

David had a great voice—informative, interesting and soothing. Jasmine hadn't realized she had closed her eyes, too—until she opened them and discovered Jacob was looking at her.

"We're on it," he said softly. "The Miami office will speak to your captain and see that the police are aware of this new player."

"I just…" Jasmine paused, looking to the front.

David was going on, talking about the development of the area for tourists. The entrepreneurs had started off developing their crops—avocado, for one—and taking tourists on day trips from the City of Miami. Then came food stands and finally, the Browns Hotel, which was still standing.

"What if this man, Connor, is…a killer?"

Jasmine asked quietly. "One of those men who can only get off if he strangles or stabs a woman. What if…?"

"He'll be followed and watched, Jasmine. And, they'll do the same with him as they did with me—just a date, first. Just a date. We'll find out about him, and Kari will be all right."

Kari would be all right. And that meant so much. But what about Mary? She'd been gone nearly a month now.

Jacob started fumbling in his pocket. She realized his phone was buzzing. He answered it in a quiet voice.

David kept speaking. "Collins needed money. He got it from the Lummus guys. He started construction of a wooden bridge. The beach areas went through a number of different names, but you can still find those founding fathers in street names here—and of course, we have Fisher Island, a haven for the very rich. If you really want to find a lot of these founders, we can do that another day.

"You should see the old Miami City Cemetery across on the mainland. It was north of the city limits in 1887 when it was founded. Julia Tuttle is buried there, and oh! If you like Civil War history, we've got some Confederates buried just feet from some Union guys—friends by then, I would think, since they died long after the war. Friends in death, if nothing else."

Jasmine looked at Jacob. He smiled tightly at her. "We have two guys on it. They're trying to dig up something on Connor, but we don't even have a first name for the man."

"He's English. He definitely had an accent."

"I told them that. Jasmine, they're watching Kari. She's at her apartment right now."

"She's an innocent… She's a Mary. She isn't worried about…about anything he might ask her to do. She said she's been with dozens of losers and might as well improve her career chances by going with men chosen for her by Kozak or Natasha. I'll never forgive myself if she gets hurt. I could have gone with Connor."

"She's going to be all right."

Jasmine nodded, taking a deep breath.

David talked on, telling them that when the South Beach area had fallen into a slump, Jackie Gleason had helped to change things doing his famous show from the beach, along with more entrepreneurs who saw the fabulous artistic value of the art deco hotels and buildings.

They were finally nearing their destination.

"The Ancient Spanish Monastery, known officially as the Monastery of St. Bernard de Clairvaux, is really—well, ancient. Construction began in northern Spain in 1133, in a little place near Segovia called Sacramenia. It housed monks for somewhere around seven hundred years, and then there was a revolution and it was sold and became a granary and storage and…not a monastery.

"It came to be here because, in 1925, it was purchased by an American—you guessed it—entrepreneur, Mr. William Randolph Hearst. For a long time, it was known as the world's biggest jigsaw puzzle, because it was shipped to the US as thousands upon thousands of stones.

"Well, then Hearst had some financial problems. He'd wanted to rebuild it at San Simeon, but some of what he'd purchased of the monastery was sold off. The crates—about eleven thousand of them—were in storage in New York. Not to mention there had been an outbreak of hoof-and-mouth disease in Segovia, which meant the packing hay had to be burned and the crates had to be quarantined.

"And then poor Hearst died! More entrepreneurs invested, and all the crates were taken out of storage. Took about a year and a half, they say, to put all the pieces back together. Two businessmen bought them, had them put together and then couldn't afford the fact that the monastery didn't make it right away as a tourist attraction. Financial difficulties again.

"In 1964, it was purchased by Bishop Henry Louttit, who gave it to the diocese of South Florida, which split into three groups. Then it was owned by a very rich and good man, a billionaire and a philanthropist, Colonel Robert Pentland, Jr. He went on that year to give the cloisters to the Bishop of Florida, and voilà! Finally, a church and a tourist attraction. And now, while the monastery is still a great tourist attraction, it's still also an active church. I love going there. It's like stepping back in time."

They arrived. David quickly arranged for their tickets, and Jasmine and Jacob were in, admiring the old stone cloisters and hearing about the historic instruments that were often used in services, seeing some of the artifacts that had come with the monastery—and the carved coats of arms and other relics that had come from other monasteries and venues around Spain.

Then they were out in the gardens, arm in arm, and Jacob was back on the phone again.

"I did get the autopsy information on Smirnoff from my Miami counterpart," Jacob told her as they strolled.

"I realize autopsies are important, but I'm pretty sure I know how Josef Smirnoff died—bullets," Jasmine said.

Jacob nodded. "Yes. But I guess he didn't know he had cancer—colon cancer. According to the ME, Smirnoff must have had it for some time without knowing. He wasn't looking at a long life, even if he'd gone for treatment."

"So, someone murdered him for nothing," Jasmine said. "Kozak was next in line anyway."

Jacob was quiet.

"You don't think it was Kozak?"

"He would just be so obvious. And he denied having anything to do with the bodies in the oil drums."

"Have they finished those autopsies?" Jasmine asked.

Jacob nodded. "They are still waiting on testing. They've gotten fingerprints on the most recent body, but the two other corpses were too decomposed. They think one of the bodies has been there several years."

"I'm assuming they're also trying to trace the oil drums and whatever remnants of clothing they can find?"

Jacob nodded. "They don't have much hope on the oil drums. They were apparently dumped by a major oil company years ago. They were headed to the closest landfill, I imagine. Nice, huh? Anyone could have picked them up."

"But you said they got fingerprints off the most recent corpse?"

He smiled. "As soon as I know, you'll know. Easy now that I've staked my claim on you."

"It does make communication between us a lot easier," Jasmine murmured.

"And hopefully keeps the wolves from baying at your door—and forcing you to show your hand." He grinned at her. "I can appear to be extremely possessive."

She was afraid that her smile was a little fluttery. Because something inside her had fluttered, as well.

His phone rang. He answered and listened intently. "Okay," he said, hanging up. He looked at Jasmine. "Apparently, Mr. Connor doesn't believe in being fashionably late Miami Beach–style. He's at Kari's apartment now."

"So, they're heading to dinner now. We should get back down there—"

"Jasmine, agents are on it."

"I know, but—"

Her phone rang then. She glanced at the number; it was the number that Captain Mac Lorenzo was using for the operation.

"Checking in—and watching out for a valuable asset," he told her.

"I'm fine," Jasmine assured him. "I'm touring the Ancient Spanish Monastery."

"I've spoken with Jorge. We're not pulling either of you out yet. But I also have strict instructions from way high above not to endanger an FBI operation."

"We're not endangering it."

"And you're not to endanger yourself," he reminded her.

"Never, sir," she told him.

"Just make sure you remember the FBI has taken the lead on this, and they're calling the shots."

"I understand." She was careful to keep any remnant of emotion from her voice.

"You're doing all right with interagency communication?"

Jasmine glanced at Jacob. "We're doing just fine, sir."

Jacob must have heard. He arched his brows in a question and reached for the phone.

"Captain Lorenzo, how do you do? Jacob Wolff. We're working on this together well. I don't think we could have planned this out any better."

Jasmine didn't hear what Captain Lorenzo said after that. Jacob handed the phone back to Jasmine and she quickly hung up.

"Thank you for that," she told Jacob.

He shrugged. "I think we are working well together."

"Yes, I guess we are."

"Hey, I'm pretty sure I would have liked you one way or the other. And I do admire your swing. That was a hell of a punch you gave me the other day."

"I didn't know—"

"Maybe that was better. That's the thing with undercover, really. Check in only when you need to or when you need help. Work everything on a need-to-know basis."

He was right, and she knew it. And she

could have said she liked him, too. But suddenly, doing so seemed to be a very dangerous part of the operation.

She liked him too much.

Liked the deep set of his eyes, the tone of his voice…the way he touched her. She'd liked the feel of his lips on hers far too much… That brief touch was still a memory that lingered and haunted.

"I still think we should head back," she said.

He looked around. "It's beautiful here. Not just the monastery, I mean South Florida."

"Yeah. But how often do you get down here?"

"I go where they send me," he told her.

She nodded and turned away. Even with the undercover operation underway, they were ships passing at sea. It was disturbing that she was coming to care about him, and almost humiliating the way that she felt…

With him, she would have gladly taken a feigned relationship anywhere.

It was one thing to discover she found him attractive. More, even. Compelling, sensual…a man with the kind of masculinity that moved beyond sense and logic and simply reached into the very core of her being.

It just didn't work to be craving his touch while on the job.

"Well, we've checked in, Jorge knows I'm all right," she said, "and Connor will have Kari on the beach somewhere soon. I'd like to get back to South Beach."

"We can do that," he said.

He took her arm and they headed back. David Hernandez was waiting for them by the limo. Jacob told David he was great, and they would use him in the future, but for the moment, they'd decided just to head back to the hotel. They were going to wander the sand by night.

Hernandez thought that was fine, and he was grateful they'd call on him again. Of course, the man would be pleased. He had the night off now with full pay.

Jasmine and Jacob were both quiet during the drive back. When they reached the cute little boutique hotel where Jacob was staying, Jasmine admired the old lobby.

"You've never been in here before?" he asked her.

She grinned. "When I was in high school, we used to come out here and prowl a few of the clubs and maybe have soda or coffee at a few of the hotels. But I think I've only stayed out here a few times. I'm a native, but that doesn't mean I know every hotel."

"It's nice. Not a chain. And the owners seem to love the deco spirit of the place. I can have coffee on the balcony every morning if I want. I can hear the sound of the surf and watch the palm trees sway—before the rest of the world wakes up and the beach becomes crowded with bodies."

She smiled. "You will see some of the most beautiful bodies in the world out here, you know."

He was quiet for a minute.

"You disagree?"

He smiled awkwardly and shrugged, and then looked at her at last. His light blue eyes seemed to caress the length of her.

Her heart, her soul, her *longing* seemed to jump to her throat.

But he quickly changed moods. "Then again, it's not just perfect bodies. You know that, of course."

"You mean old and wrinkly? We'll all be there someday. I hope when I'm older and drooping everywhere, I still love the beach."

He laughed. "I'm with you on that. I hope

when I'm creased and drooping everywhere I can still sit on the sand and watch the sway of the palms and not worry that someone is judging me. I believe everyone has to do what is comfortable for them—and that's part of what I love.

"Yes, there's beauty. Yes, there's the ridiculous. And there are quiet times, when the sun is rising, when you can look out and feel you're in a private paradise. And then you turn around and the neon of the hotels and the rush of the world comes on in. This place is ever changing, plastic in so many ways and yet real when it comes to the feel of the salt air and those moments when you're in the water, and it's just you and the waves and the sea and the sky."

"Yes," she said softly.

"So, let's take a walk," he said.

They headed out to the beach. Jasmine doffed her sneakers and Jacob rid himself of his shoes and socks, too. They left them by a palm.

Jacob's phone rang.

He listened, and then he told Jasmine, "Connor has Kari out to dinner. He took her to Joe's Stone Crab. They're fine."

"I'm afraid for when they leave. What do we do now?"

"Wait," he said.

"So hard!"

He laughed. "I've been undercover for months at a time. Watching, waiting. And for this case, well, the watching and waiting is a hell of a lot better than usual." He was quiet for a minute. "I recently worked a case where immigrants were brought in and used horribly. It was long on my part, but when it broke, we moved quickly. This may be the same. Thing is, right now, we could get them, or Ivan at least, on money. Then again, they can employ the best legal team known to man. So, we have to take them down big-time—with evidence that prosecutors can take to court."

Jasmine muttered, "So…we wait."

"And play the part," he agreed.

Nightfall was coming in earnest. The sky was fighting darkness and the sun was shooting out rays that seemed to be pure gold and magenta.

Jasmine wasn't sure what got into her. She suddenly broke away from him and ran down the beach, turned and kicked up a spray of the waves that had been washing over their feet.

She caught him with a full body splash, and he yelped and laughed with surprise. Then he came after her.

She squealed and turned to run, but he tackled her and bore her down to the soft damp sand. He leaned over her, looked down into her eyes and then murmured, "Good move. I just saw Sasha up on the boardwalk. We are being watched."

He eased closer. "Can I kiss you?"

Role-playing…

She tangled her fingers into the richness of his hair, pulling him in, and he kissed her.

And then he broke away, laughing, and pulled her to her feet. "I think we gave Sasha a good show, eh?" he asked softly.

"Oh, yeah," she whispered. Once again, her lips were burning.

As they retrieved their shoes and decided on a restaurant for dinner, she couldn't help but wish that the FBI had sent down a much less attractive agent.

Chapter Seven

"His full name is Donald McPherson Connor," Jacob told Jasmine. "He's living at that grand old place down from the club just off of Washington Street—a quiet and dark intersection. The whole sixth floor is his apartment."

They were at her place. He'd done a thorough search for bugs and hadn't found any, and with the way this gang seemed to work, he was pretty sure he wouldn't find anything. In Kozak's words, Jasmine was "just a woman."

Jacob had a feeling that Kozak might be pretty surprised.

Just a woman. In any kind of a fair fight, Jasmine would take Kozak.

But for them, at this moment, it bode well that Kozak and the members of his gang still seemed to live in an archaic world of chauvinism.

"And what else?" Jasmine asked.

"Born in Yorkshire, and he has dual citizenship."

"How does he make his money?"

"He inherited a nice sum and knows how to invest in the stock market."

"So, an older Englishman-turned-American, rich, with nothing to do. Wife? Kids?"

Jasmine had changed from her salt-spray-and-sand-covered clothing to a dark silky maxi dress. She'd come to perch on the sofa by him, hugging her knees to her chest as she looked at him.

"Wife died about ten years ago. They had a daughter but I can't find much on her."

"Criminal past?"

"Nope."

"Any hint of anyone disappearing when he's around?"

"He's been living in Savannah. He's just been down here about two months. They're still looking into him."

"And the agent saw him take Kari back to her apartment and then leave?"

"Yes," Jacob said.

He didn't have to read from his phone; one of his assets was his memory. He could retain what was told to him, which was probably why languages came to him easily. Then again, he loved languages, and all the little rules and differences and nuances within them.

He wished at that moment, though, that he was reading. Because he was left to meet her eyes.

He'd been right that first day, when he'd seen her from afar. Her eyes were green. A brilliant beautiful green, like twin emeralds in a sea of gold. Her face was so perfectly molded he was tempted to reach out and touch it, as he might be tempted to reach out and touch a classic sculpture. Her hair was free, freshly washed and tumbling around her shoulders, still damp. And in the maxi dress, she seemed exceptionally alluring—though he was sure she had donned the article of clothing because it covered her entire body. It felt like a reaction to the skimpy outfit she'd been forced to put on for the "date" with Connor.

"But according to Kari, Mary did escort him," Jasmine pointed out, "and then she disappeared."

"You're going to need to get closer to Kari."

"Well, we're both supposed to report to Natasha tomorrow—Kari and I."

"And I have an excuse to go in. I've gotten Kozak's permission to investigate Smirnoff's murder."

"Have the cops gotten anything? I guess not. I'm pretty sure that, even though the FBI has lead, I'd know about it if anyone had been apprehended for the murder."

"From what I've heard, they're still pretty much in the dark," Jacob said. "Trajectory shows the bullets were fired from the balcony. But everyone working there swears the balconies were closed off. Someone is lying, of course. But no one knows who."

"No guns were found, no casings…no nothing?"

"Nope. And the gunmen—two to three of them, best estimate—entirely disappeared."

Jasmine leaned her chin thoughtfully on her knees. "We could see all the major players when it happened. You were out there with Kozak, Ivan Petrov and the goons, Sasha, Antonio and Alejandro. And Natasha was backstage."

"The killers were hired, obviously. And they were guaranteed a clean getaway. We dusted for prints on the rails and so forth, but there are hundreds of prints. Workmen were there, of course, before the grand opening. Anyone who so much as delivered pizza might have left a print. Smirnoff, from what I understand, loved showing off the place and brought everyone out to those balconies to let them see how they looked down at the floor and the main stage."

She shook her head. "So, we're nowhere."

"No. We're moving forward. You're just impatient."

"I guess so. I mean, I have worked undercover before. But often just for a day or so, getting into the right place, talking to the right people. I admit—it was never anything like this."

"We just keep moving forward."

She nodded. "I guess… I guess I need some sleep."

"Go on."

"You're staying here?"

"I believe I'm entitled now—and I don't want to disappoint anyone by not taking my full measure."

"Ah." She stood, almost leaping away from him. "Pillow and blankets. If I'd known I was having nightly guests, I would have asked for a two-bedroom." She smiled awkwardly and hurried into her bedroom. A moment later, she was back. She plopped down two pillows, sheets and a blanket. "Not sure if you need the blanket, I don't air-condition the place too much. But… Anyway, all right. I'll see you in the morning. Start coffee if you're up first!"

She spoke quickly, almost nervously. It wasn't like her.

"Good night," he said softly.

She left him, and he wished he wasn't playing a role. More than that, he wished he wasn't working. She'd closed the door between them, but he could still see her in his mind's eye.

See her laughter as she kicked up the salt spray.

Feel her beneath him when he tackled her in the sand.

He could see the emerald of her eyes as she'd looked at him before she pulled him in for that blistering kiss.

And he couldn't help but wonder, in his misery, if she just might…just might…be wishing a little bit herself that they had met under different circumstances.

He spent the next hour reminding himself he was a special agent, he loved his job and he had made a difference… They were professional. They played their parts. They brought down the bad guys.

He thought he'd never sleep. He wondered why the hell he had stayed. She could take care of herself. She was trained.

But despite the logic, despite what he knew, he was afraid for her.

He could have returned to his apartment. He knew being here had nothing to do with being professional. If it came to it, he'd give anything to save her life if it was threatened in any way.

Why? He'd worked cases with so many beautiful women and never done more than acknowledge that fact.

Jasmine was different. She had touched something else in him. Something that was more than attraction, even desire.

She was...everything. Everything in a way he hadn't known in over a decade. Not since his wife had died.

JACOB WAS UP when Jasmine emerged in the morning.

She'd spent the night...waiting. She'd thought the door to her bedroom might open at any time. She couldn't decide if she wanted it to or not.

But it did not, and when she finally rose, she found him already awake. He'd brewed coffee and was sipping a cup, leaning thoughtfully against the refrigerator.

He looked at her as she emerged, his eyes fathomless.

"Three more bodies last night," he said softly.

"What? Where?" she asked. Three bodies. Was one Mary?

He must have seen the fear on her face. "Three men again," he said quickly. "And they weren't found in oil drums. This time, they were found south of the Tamiami Trail. Miami-Dade County, on Miccosukee tribal land."

"Three. Maybe the hired gunmen? If they weren't in oil drums, if they're new... It's possible it isn't related. Will we get identities soon?" Jasmine said.

He hesitated. "No. The bodies are missing heads and hands."

"Oh."

"Cause of death?"

"Unknown, at this point. In my mind, logic suggests they were shot in the head."

"Logic?"

"Execution-style—then the heads were removed. Dumped them in the Everglades." He hesitated. "From what I've been told, they were well ravaged by the animal life. Among other creatures, the vultures had a feast."

"There are few better places to dispose of a body than the Everglades," Jasmine agreed. "But they were definitely...male bodies?"

"Yes, definitely male bodies."

She wandered to the coffeepot and poured herself a cup. She was shaken, but she didn't want to be. She was a detective in a major crime division. But this was personal.

Maybe she shouldn't have been working this investigation. But there had truly been no one better suited to the task of getting in with the Deco Gang.

Jacob came up behind her and placed a hand on her shoulders. "Jasmine, I believe the men found might well have been the shooters. If whoever planned this wanted to make sure no one talked, they had to get rid of the people who actually carried out the deed."

"Yes, that's my gut feeling on it, too," she said. Her hands were still trembling slightly as she held her coffee cup. And she was ridiculously aware of him, right there behind her, the heat of his body, the scent of him.

She had to spin around, composed and determined. "So, today, you start questioning everyone?"

"Today I start questioning everyone."

He had barely spoken when there was a knock on the door.

"Excuse me," she murmured.

As she headed to the door, she was aware Jacob had already showered and dressed completely for the day. He had his hand behind his back, ready to draw his weapon if the guest at the door intended to offer any danger.

No danger was forthcoming; she looked through the peephole. It was Jorge.

She let him in quickly. "Hey."

Jorge glanced at Jacob. He seemed to accept the man's presence as normal.

"I was bringing you the latest news. Captain said he didn't think you should be calling in, even on the burners. Too easy for one of them to catch the phone and check out numbers and get suspicious when nothing on you had an easily trackable number. But I imagine you've gotten the latest?"

"The bodies in the Glades?" she asked.

He nodded and looked at Jacob. "Who do you think did it? Is it Kozak? Natasha? Ivan?"

"I don't know. But I intend to find out." Jacob smiled. "Breakfast first. Somewhere obvious. Somewhere anyone who wishes can see the three of us—me and my escort, provided for me with their blessing, and you, my new love's best friend. Plenty of places in the area. Let's go for a walk and find good food."

"Okay," Jorge said slowly, frowning.

"Then Jasmine needs to check in with Natasha and assure her of my happiness and her own satisfaction with the arrangement—and I get to question the goons."

"And…" Jorge pressed. "Me?"

"I think it's fine if you come in today, just a cheerful dude happy to be with a friend."

"It's a plan," Jorge said.

IT WASN'T DIFFICULT for Jacob to pretend to be out with friends. He liked Jorge very much and thought he was probably a damned good cop. He knew how to fit in to what he was doing, and he didn't need to take the lead. He'd set up the tour for them yesterday in minutes flat and had managed to introduce him and Jasmine on the floor opening night at the club—at the end of a spray of bullets—without giving things away. Jacob also just liked the man.

And as for Jasmine…

He had to be careful.

When they were seated, Jasmine and Jorge were talking about Miami, and Jasmine was telling Jorge about their tour guide.

"He was a great guy—a super guide, knew his stuff," Jasmine said. "Friendly and informative without being annoying."

"Hard to imagine this place as a coconut plantation," Jacob said.

"Hard to imagine the whole south of the state as a 'river of grass,'" Jasmine said.

Jacob noted that there was a man seated at a far back table, eating and reading a newspaper. Watching them.

Jacob picked up his coffee cup and said softly, "Antonio Garibaldi is at the back of the restaurant."

"We were followed here," Jorge said casually.

"And here's the thing," Jasmine said, running her fingers up Jacob's arm and smiling sensually, "we don't even know who else might be in the employ of the new boss, be he Kozak or even someone else."

Jacob leaned closer to her. "We need to find out who is calling the shots." He planted a quick kiss on her lips and looked at her lingeringly. Then he stood. "Think I'll visit the restroom."

He headed to the back of the restaurant and the restrooms. But he made a pretense of stopping, as if surprised and pleased to see Garibaldi.

"Hey! I guess I did choose a good place, if you're here," he said. He pulled out the chair on the other side of the table and sat.

"Yeah, they do a great breakfast," Garibaldi said. He was a big man with dark hair and a solid physique, built as a good bouncer should be. His eyes were quick and dark. His smile was pained.

"I'm really loving South Florida," Jacob told him. "And getting to work with Kozak. Of course, I'm as sympathetic as anyone over Smirnoff. He was a good man. What the hell do you think happened? I mean, forgive me, I know you guys are good at your jobs. But how the hell did shooters get up on the balconies?"

Garibaldi looked uncomfortable—he was on the spot. Then he leaned forward. "Hell if I know. Seriously. From the beginning, it was planned that the balconies be roped off. Crowd control. And that day… Smirnoff was giving us our orders. I was watching the front, Suarez had the stage and Antonovich was moving through the crowd. There were cops all over, hired for the occasion. I'll be damned if I can figure it out, and I've tried. Thing is, I was given my orders. The other guys were given their orders. We never saw anyone get up there."

"There has to be an entrance from the offices," Jacob said.

"Sure. There's a door across from Smirnoff's office. That way, when he chose to, he could be in his office, and when he wanted to be part of the crowd, he could come out on the balcony. The cops were all over it. But here's the thing. The door is kept locked. There's a key. And when the cops were all over the place right after the shooting, the door was still locked. Smirnoff kept the key."

"Duplicate keys can be made. I'm sure the cops checked on that," Jacob said.

Garibaldi shrugged. "Whoever may have had a duplicate key, I don't know."

"It was obviously well planned."

Garibaldi appeared to be honestly confused. "You know, sure, it could have been planned. But it seemed like one of those bad things, you know. Some disturbed person just out to hurt anyone—and getting Smirnoff."

"You don't believe that, do you?" Jacob asked.

Garibaldi's voice was soft and low. "I want to believe it," he said.

"But you don't."

"Kozak told us last night that he'd given you permission to question us, see if you couldn't figure something out. I'd like to help you. What do I know? I was in my position. And the shooting started. I was—well, hell. Hate to admit this. I was scared. I think I managed to get people out, get them down. But I got the hell out as fast as I could myself."

"You were armed?"

"I was. But the best gun in the world doesn't do you a bit of good if you don't know what you're supposed to be shooting at."

He seemed to be telling the truth. Jacob never took anyone at face value, but he also noted the man's expressions and body language. He'd have bet that he was being honest.

Garibaldi looked at him and seemed to judge him, as well. "I'm not in this for violence," he said softly. "The money is good…" He shrugged. "I mind my own business and don't care where it comes from. Drugs… People are going to buy them somewhere. The girls… They do what they choose. Natasha talked to Jasmine, and you all had an agreement. Cool. She seems to really like you. So, is that a crime? As for me, I do what I'm told and I keep my nose clean and stay out. I'm just security."

"So you're just supposed to report on us today?" Jacob asked him.

"Yeah. And it's cool. It's obvious you two have more than a business relationship going. That's the way Josef Smirnoff always rolled. Kozak said that it will be business as usual. Of course, he's scared now. Whoever killed Smirnoff could be gunning for him. That's probably why he said you could talk to people. Though, I already told the cops what I told you. The truth."

"Sure. Hey, next time you're watching us, just join us." Jacob shrugged. "She's a cool girl and I like Jorge, too."

"That wouldn't be the way the game is played," Garibaldi said.

"No, I guess not." Jacob stood. "You're a good-looking man with the right stuff. There are tons of other places on the beach that need bouncers, security. If this whole scene is too much for you."

Garibaldi shrugged. "I screwed up once. Didn't check an ID the way I should have. The girl's parents caused a stink. Josef gave me a job. Said I didn't need to ID anyone." He laughed suddenly. "Garibaldi. Nice Italian name. I was born here, my parents were born here and my grandfather came over from Naples to run a tailor shop. No mob ties whatsoever. He was in Worcester, Massachusetts. And didn't even have to pay anyone for a safe working environment.

"Alejandro Suarez, his family came over in the late 1880s. They were cigar makers up in Ybor City, Tampa area. And even Antonovich, he's a third-generation American. We're not… we're not mob. We're not mob-related. I'm here because I have a job. And I do it. Long hours, maybe, but so far, I haven't been asked to do anything other than protect people, watch people and break up fights."

"And what if you had to do something that was illegal?"

"It would depend on what that thing was." Garibaldi hesitated a minute. Then he said quietly, "Hey, man, you're buying art—that you haven't even seen. And we all know about your past."

Jacob nodded. "Yeah. But I play it the way Smirnoff played it. I don't go in for murder. Gets messy—and gets the cops on you."

"Yeah," Garibaldi agreed.

"Sounds like you're a good man. One I'd like to have on my side," Jacob said.

"Thanks," Garibaldi told him.

Jacob left him and returned to his own table. Jasmine and Jorge were having a conversation about the best spas in the area. When he sat down, Jasmine played it perfectly, stroking his arm.

He wished her touch didn't seem to awaken every ounce of longing in his body.

NATASHA WAS WITH Kozak when they arrived.

Jacob was allowed admittance to Kozak's office. Jasmine and Jorge were directed to the dressing room, where they were alone.

Jorge found a stereo system and turned on music. Phil Collins, "In the Air Tonight." Fitting. Shades of the old *Miami Vice* that had really put the area—and many myths about it—on the map.

"Natasha is sleeping with Kozak," Jorge said

softly. "She might have been sleeping with Josef Smirnoff, too. At any rate, she was with him for years and years. Trusted. She could have gotten the key and had a copy made."

Natasha came sweeping into the room. She saw Jorge and frowned slightly, then shrugged. "I suppose you say anything in front of Jorge," she said. "Oh, by the way, Jorge, a man has been courting our business, one who may need some entertainment."

"Ready when you are," Jorge said.

"Now, Jasmine, about Mr. Marensky…"

Jasmine smiled and then decided to go another step. She walked over and hugged Natasha.

The woman was not used to hugs. She didn't push Jasmine away, but she didn't hug her back. She awkwardly patted her shoulders. "So, all went well," Natasha said.

"He's lovely," Jasmine said. "Best way to make some money I've ever known!"

"Yes, I believe you. You're very lucky such a man is so captivated by you. It's not always the case, but for you… Yes, I am glad that such a striking man—one whom Josef approved and Victor seems to admire, especially—has taken such a shine to you. But you must realize, my dear, he may tire of you. And move on."

"I know that," Jasmine said. "But for now... he's fun. He wishes to please me."

"And he is far from repulsive in bed, I imagine," Natasha said.

Jasmine didn't let her smile slip. "Oh, so, so, far from repulsive."

"Ah, she's a lucky one," Jorge said.

"Then you will continue as you have been doing. Don't forget... Friday night. Friday is the funeral. And at the funeral, you will be a hostess here, and you mustn't cling to Mr. Marensky at the gathering after the ceremony. After tomorrow night, the club may reopen. The workers will have cleaned up. No bullet holes will show in the walls by the ceremony. Now, you do understand about Marensky, Jasmine? First, we need you to be working. Second, it's important he remembers that he is graced with your company through us."

"Definitely," Jasmine said. "Understood."

"Then you are free for today. You may go. You, too, Jorge." She handed them each an envelope. Their paychecks. They had no choice but to thank her and leave.

As they walked, they noted they were being

followed. It was Alejandro Suarez on their tail this time.

"So, straight to my place, I guess," Jasmine murmured.

"I don't think they're following me."

"What about phones?"

"I have a new one."

"I need to know about Connor. About Connor…and Kari."

Jorge sighed. "Jasmine, we have to trust our fellows. They saw last night that Connor left Kari at her apartment. No sex, nothing. She was fine."

Aware of their follower, Jasmine laughed as if Jorge had said something great and grabbed his arm in fun—as a friend might do. In contrast to her actions, her whisper was intense. "But what are they doing about him?"

"Watching. And waiting," Jorge said. "Jasmine, you knew this wasn't going to be an instant fix, that we'd be out of the loop much of the time. And—"

They had only come a half a block from the club when Jasmine saw Kari headed their way. She released Jorge's arm and cried out with delight, running to see the other girl.

"Kari!" She hugged her. She pulled away and asked softly, "All is well?"

"Fine, it's lovely. Mr. Connor is an absolute gentleman. I'll be seeing him tonight." Kari grinned and said, "Oh, he isn't young and hot like Marensky. But he's fine, very nice. Polite and courteous in a way I haven't seen in years. Happy to have some arm candy while he's out on the town, you know?"

"Good. Well, I guess you knew that, from what Mary said."

"I miss Mary. She was the sweetest!"

"Did she ever say anything to you," Jasmine asked, "anything about going away or even… even about being afraid?"

"No. She was just with us, and then one day she didn't show and didn't come back. Natasha was very upset. She was very fond of Mary, too. Speaking of Natasha, I've got to get in. She wants to see me." But suddenly, Kari gripped Jasmine's hands. "I'm telling you, Mr. Connor is so kind and caring, wanting to know my every wish."

Jasmine realized then that it was the man's very kindness that actually frightened Kari.

Someone so nice. What happened when he wasn't? What might he really want?

Further determined, Jasmine smiled. "Great, Kari," she said loudly. "I guess Jorge and I are going to go home and binge on repeats of *Desperate Housewives*."

"Have fun!"

"You're welcome to join us!"

Kari waved and headed off.

Jasmine headed back and grabbed Jorge's arm. "Something has to be done," she said firmly. "Before tonight!"

Chapter Eight

"I have had that door rekeyed," Kozak told Jacob. "The police asked about it, but it was locked. There was no sign that anyone had forced it. But…how? How did someone get through the balcony without being seen? There were dressers here, makeup artists… But when the show began, everyone was downstairs. Natasha was with the girls backstage. The band members were all downstairs. I didn't have the key! No one had the key—except for Josef Smirnoff."

"Someone obviously copied it," Jacob said flatly.

Kozak shook his head. "I have the only key now. No one knows where I keep it. And I don't intend to tell anyone. Including you. No offense or disrespect intended."

"None taken," Jacob said.

"You are free to look around, but I have to go. Josef's body is at the funeral home. I will make sure he is given the send-off such a man deserves."

"Where will the funeral be?"

"A small Russian Orthodox church, up the way on the beach. And then we will come here." Kozak hesitated. "Will you make the arrangements for it with me today?"

"I thought that I should stay here. We want to know what happened to Josef," Jacob reminded him.

"We do." Kozak sighed deeply. "Yes, you must speak with Antonio, Alejandro and Sasha. The thing is..."

"What is it?"

"They have their place. We work carefully. Of course, they are aware... But we never give them facts. They know people, they know who is important, but we have never given them much on the clients."

"They might have seen something," Jacob said. "Something they don't even know they saw. I've spoken with Antonio. You didn't tell me about the door and the key."

"I didn't. I had to make sure. Josef brought you in, and he assured me you were solid, that you were a powerful man with a long history. I had to come to know you myself." Kozak shrugged. "The police checked the door. They remain with nothing."

"But you know someone within your own ranks had to be involved."

Kozak looked unhappy. "Yes. But whoever did this, they were clever. They hired out. A man doesn't guard what he doesn't see to be in danger."

"No," Jacob agreed, trying to read Kozak.

"You must do what you will. I have hidden nothing on Josef's murder from the police. I will not hide it from you. But I must prepare to bury an old and dear friend."

It was evident that Kozak wanted company while he made arrangements at the funeral home. Perhaps it was even important to go with him.

"I will go with you," Jacob agreed.

As it turned out, Kozak didn't want a driver with them. He had a big black Cadillac sedan, and he asked Jacob if he would do the driving.

"You don't want one of the guys to come along?"

"A bodyguard?" Kozak asked. "I think you will do."

They took Collins Avenue north and reached the funeral home. They were greeted by a solemn man in a suit, Mr. Derby, the current owner of Sacred Night Final Rest Parlor.

Derby expressed his condolences, offered them water or coffee and then tactfully suggested they needed to choose a coffin. The coffins ranged from a few thousand dollars to just about enough to buy a house—at the least, a nice automobile.

Jacob was surprised to see tears in Victor Kozak's eyes. He had either really cared for his friend, or he was able to pull off a feat many a Hollywood actor could not.

Then again, business was business. He could have loved the man—and still arranged for his death.

"What do you think, my friend?" Kozak asked Jacob.

"Personally?" Jacob asked. "I believe in a greater power, but I don't believe the body is anything but a shell. It makes no difference if a man is laid to rest in the finest mahogany or the cheapest pine, or if he's cremated and his ashes thrown to the wind. But if you're worried about the funeral, about our show of respect…then I'd say this."

Mr. Derby, the funeral director, was eyeing Jacob with anything but kindness. Still, he seemed to perk up when Jacob pointed out a fairly expensive coffin, one that was both handsome, staid and possessed just the right amount of ornamentation.

"Perfect," Kozak said quietly. "This one is it, sir."

"All right, nice choice," Mr. Derby said. "Now, as to the wake—"

"No wake," Kozak said. "You will bring the body to the church. Closed coffin."

"Sir, my people have done an extraordinary job. You may have a wake. Mr. Smirnoff's face was not impacted, and his suit will cover—"

"No wake. No open coffin," Kozak said. "Josef will be honored and buried."

"As you wish, sir. As you wish. This is a painful time for you as a friend. I do suggest that you consider a viewing, for other friends—"

"No," Kozak said. "Our business is quite complete. We have our own cars for the services. You will bring Josef as arranged to the church. And arrange for the transport from there to the cemetery."

"Yes, Mr. Kozak. Arrangements have been

made. He will be brought from the church to the cemetery. Now, the cemetery is over in Miami. You will need police officers for the journey as friends follow for the last services, something which, of course, we take care of for you."

Kozak waved a hand in the air. "Do what is needed."

He was anxious to leave; Jacob held back and assured Derby, "Someone will be by with the final check."

He then followed Victor Kozak back out to the car. The man waited by the passenger's side as Jacob clicked the door open.

Kozak was trembling when he sat. Jacob hurried around to the driver's seat. He didn't have to push; Kozak appeared ready to speak.

"It's not real—I was there. I was there for a hail of bullets. I watched my friend fall, I saw the blood. And yet, it's not real. Not until you see he is laid into the ground. Yes, it is indeed a hard time. You know this. You have laid a wife to rest."

Jacob was still a moment.

A deceased wife was in his fake dossier. It was always best, when creating such a lie, to incorporate many details of life that were real. That helped an agent live the lie that was being created.

"It was a long time ago, right?" Victor Kozak asked.

Yes, a lifetime ago. He'd fallen in love with Sabrina Marshall the minute he had seen her. It had been tenth grade. They'd quickly become an item; he, a high school jock, Sabrina the smart one. They'd married and gone off to college together, and even after graduation when they'd planned their perfect life, talked about starting a family...

The cancer had found her. It had cared nothing about youthful dreams.

"It was a long time ago, yes," Jacob said softly.

A long, long time ago. Many women in between; savvy, bright women, some in business, some in politics, but none in law enforcement.

None like Jasmine, someone he had seen from afar who had nevertheless seemed to enter into his soul. He barely knew her. Maybe, though, he knew her enough.

Maybe, when this was over... When this was all over, Jasmine would no longer be playing a role. She would go back to her passion, being cop in a major crime unit. And he would go where the Bureau sent him, because he was good at what he did, and he did believe, no matter what unbelievable things were going on in the world, that what he did was right. One good man, or maybe many good men, could make the world a better place.

Sabrina had believed that, too.

"I'm sorry," Kozak said.

"So am I," Jacob said softly. "So am I."

"But now, this woman, this Jasmine—she means something to you?"

"Yes," Jacob said simply.

"When Natasha brought her in, I knew, too, there was something about her. Women…most often, they are just part of business, and that's how it must be. So few have that inner fire. But, now and then…one enchants the mind, eh?"

"Yes," Jacob agreed. "This one in particular…there is something that appeals to me on many levels."

"She's all yours," Kozak said.

Jacob lowered his head. He was pretty sure he knew how Jasmine would feel about being granted to a man as payment for his friendship.

Heading back to Washington Street, Jacob cut down Meridian Avenue. As they neared the Holocaust Memorial of the Greater Miami Jewish Federation, Kozak made a little sound.

The memorial was a heart-wrenching, well-conceived artwork, created by survivors, respected and honored by a community. Statues and plaques told a story that tore at the human soul.

Jacob had been there several times through the years. His own past was a checkered piece of all manner of peoples, from the free world and from areas of great subjugation; his Russian mother had a background that included royalty, his Israeli father had parents who had barely made it out of Germany. Jacob was eternally grateful they had chosen the United States as a place to raise their own family—he knew he'd had a relatively easy and privileged start to life.

He was surprised when Kozak asked him to stop.

"You want to get out and walk around?" Jacob asked.

Kozak shook his head. "I just want to look."

Jacob sat next to him in silence.

"World War II. A brutal business. Hitler wanting to exterminate a race of people. Stalin…twenty million Russians were also killed, you know, between the enemy and Stalin."

"Yes, I am aware."

"Young people these days…they don't always know."

"Education is everything," Jacob murmured.

One of the sculptures at the outdoor memorial was especially poignant. It depicted a body, as many bodies had been found. Prisoners had not just gone to the death camps to be gassed and cremated; they'd gone to be a work force, and they'd been all but starved as they worked.

The body was skeletal and depicted in bronze. They were a distance from the sculpture and couldn't see it completely. But Jacob had seen it before. And he knew that Kozak had, too.

Kozak turned to Jacob. "My grandmother survived by hiding in plain sight in Berlin. My grandfather was a Russian soldier, hiding the fact that he was also Jewish. When the Soviet Army closed in on Berlin, my grandfather found my grandmother, who was terrified. She had been in living with a Christian German couple who were appalled by the death and terror around them. She'd been told, however, there was less torture if you quickly admitted what you were. When he found her, she said, *'Juden.'* But you see, my grandfather said, *'Juden*, yes, I am *Juden*, too.' They were married, and they stayed married for the next forty years. They died in the same year. I believe he died of a broken heart when he lost her, because she passed away first."

"They had years together. It is still a beautiful story," Jacob said.

Kozak turned to him. "I have told you this story because maybe it will help you believe me. I don't kill people. I don't torture, and I don't kill."

Jacob couldn't help himself. Looking at Kozak, he said, "I beg to differ—slightly. Drugs kill."

Kozak waved a hand in the air. "Drugs kill, but people have a choice. But we do nothing where others have not made a choice. The addict must choose life. The drugs exist with or without my participation. We may as well get rich. Am I a good man? No. Am I a cold-blooded killer? No. Take what you will from that. But I did not kill my friend Josef."

Jacob nodded slowly.

Neither spoke for a moment.

He put the car back into gear and drove back south, to Washington Street and the club. They hadn't been away long.

"So, now," Kozak said, "you will find out what happened to Josef, yes?"

"I will do my damnedest," Jacob said.

JORGE REALLY DID put on a Netflix marathon of *Desperate Housewives*.

Jasmine nervously paced the room. "We should be doing something," she said.

"Jasmine, here's the thing. We are doing something," Jorge told her. "Okay, so, you're not a fan. What should we watch?"

"I can't. I can't sit still."

"You stink at this."

"Sorry!"

"All right," Jorge said. "I'll check in with Captain Lorenzo. Will that help?"

"Maybe."

He took out his phone and called. Jasmine watched him as he spoke, assuring Lorenzo they were both fine and they were proceeding with the work and their relationship with the FBI was moving along smoothly. Then he asked if anything else had been discovered, listened a while and then thanked Lorenzo and promised he'd be the one in touch.

"Well?" Jasmine demanded, burning with impatience.

"There's a Miccosukee village where they sell handmade clothing, arts and crafts—and have alligator shows," he said.

"I know. It's out on Tamiami Trail, just west of Shark Valley."

"There's a fellow who lives not far from the village. He raises alligators, sells them to various venues for alligator wrestling. Handles them from the time they hatch." Jorge stopped speaking.

"And?"

"One of his young alligators died, and he didn't know why, so there was a necropsy done on the gator."

"And?"

"They found a hand. He reported it. And it's been brought in to the medical examiner, and they believe it belonged to one of the dead men found out there. They're hoping to get an ID. I don't know a lot about alligator stomach acids, but…well, they're still hoping to get something."

"I know what they're going to find," Jasmine said. "There won't be a match. I'm willing to bet that whoever is doing this is clever enough to have hired undocumented newcomers to do the deed."

"Maybe. Someone desperate and grateful for any work that doesn't go on the books."

Jasmine nodded. "Jorge, what do you think of Natasha?"

"She's all business."

"Yes. And she was in charge of the models. Of the show. And we all suspect she is sleeping with Victor Kozak, but—"

"Maybe she slept with Josef, too. And maybe she was sleeping with Victor because Josef tired of her, and maybe—"

"Maybe!" Jasmine said. "If only we had a definite."

She started to pace again, thinking, trying to remember every move Natasha had made on the day of the show.

Jorge groaned and turned back to *Desperate Housewives*.

"Hey," Jacob said to Alejandro Suarez. He was on guard downstairs, at the door to the club offices and staging area.

"Hey," Suarez said. He studied Jacob. He

was puffing on a cigarette, leaned against the wall. He grinned suddenly. "Are you some new kind of enforcer?"

"I'm just an art dealer."

Suarez studied him. "Sure. But hey, I just work here. Kozak said you were going to talk to us."

"Do you remember anyone—anyone you didn't know—at the grand opening?"

Suarez laughed. "Anyone I didn't know? What? Do I look like I rub elbows with the rich and famous regularly?" There must have been something ominous in Jacob's look, because he quickly sobered up.

"Did you see anyone upstairs?" Jacob clarified. "We know that the killers were on the balcony."

"Yeah, that's what the cops said." Suarez sighed, reaching in his jacket pocket for another cigarette. He lit it with his current smoke. The man was a few years younger than Garibaldi and maybe a few inches taller in height. "I came in through the upstairs. We all reported to Josef, who said the balcony would be closed off. That would leave all of us down on the floor with the hired cops—you don't do anything that big without hiring cops."

"Right."

"When I checked in, the girls were all getting dressed. The band members were in the green room, making cracks about the girls. I guess they planned on having them in to party later. That idea went all to hell, huh?"

"You saw the band, Josef Smirnoff, Natasha and the girls. Anyone else?"

"Ivan was already down at the bar. The caterers were never allowed upstairs. Oh, Victor Kozak was downstairs already when I came in, seeing to a last-minute check on the place. When I joined him, he pointed out that the balcony stairways—there's one set near the entrance on both sides—were roped off with velvet cords. They didn't want people up on the balcony. There's only one door up on the second floor, but it almost leads right into the office, and they didn't want anyone going up because of the office. And he didn't want anybody trying to grab selfies with the girls or the band or anything. If anyone headed toward the stairs, we were to politely stop them. And if they tried again, we were to politely escort them out."

"But no one tried to get up the stairs?"

"There were big signs attached to the velvet

cords that said No Admittance. I think most people honor signs like that. Hey, it wasn't supposed to be... It was supposed to be a cool grand opening. No one expected any violence. If anything, we'd have had to throw out a drunk."

"But you saw no one. Nothing?"

Suarez shook his head. "No! I mean, I could have told you before the cops did their investigating that the shooters had to have been on the balcony. But there was a stampede. You know that. I admit, I froze for a second. Then I went to work getting people out."

"Was anyone on the back door—where we are now?"

"I'm assuming it was locked up tight. We were all on the main floor. But..."

"But?"

"I don't know what weapons were used. I was thinking that whoever was up there... Well, if they pocketed their weapons, in all the confusion, they might have come down the stairs and run out with everyone else. Or..." Suarez paused, shaking his head.

"What?"

"They could have come out the back, out of this door. But you see, I don't understand how that would be possible. Cops were already in here. They were crawling all over the area within minutes. I can't believe they wouldn't have seen three men with guns run out this door." Suarez seemed as mystified as Garibaldi had been.

Two down; one to go.

They were great liars—or they had planned their stories well.

Jacob thanked him, then turned and hurried back up the stairs. He found Sasha Antonovich outside the door to Kozak's office. Like Alejandro Suarez, he seemed at ease—bored, probably—as he stood by the door.

"My turn, eh?" Antonovich asked him. He shrugged. "We just look stupid. Kozak said you were going to try to do what the police seem be failing at. So. What can I tell you?"

"What *can* you tell me?"

Antonovich was older than both Suarez and Garibaldi. Remembering all the info he had been given, Jacob knew Antonovich had been with Josef Smirnoff the longest—well over a decade. His hair was beginning to gray, just at the temples. Fine lines were appearing around his light brown eyes, and he wore a weary look.

The man shook his head, his expression grim. "What do I know? That it wasn't just a random shooting? That someone was after Josef? I'm sure you believe that, too. How the hell did they get in? They had to have been on a guest list. I don't know who they were, what they looked like... There were hundreds of people here. They could have been with the caterers, they could have gotten in with the off-duty cops. The cops came from all over the city. Some of them, the Miami Beach guys, were naturally on duty, but in here... Josef wanted lots of security, so we hired people from all over the city. I've been thinking about it, too."

"A dirty cop? Is that what you're thinking?"

"Maybe. Or just someone dressed up like a cop. The other guys might not have known—they came from precincts all over the city. I keep thinking, though, that the guys investigating the shooting had to have thought of all this."

"I imagine they have. I would think they're working all angles."

"Three bodies found down off the Tamiami Trail—no hands, no heads. Sure as hell sounds like a hit to me."

"I agree. I'll bet just about all of law enforcement would."

"Definitely not just a domestic disturbance," Antonovich said, not amused at his own attempt at humor. "The door up here... I was the first one to check it, along with one of Miami Beach's finest. It was locked. If they came through that way, they had a key."

"It's been rekeyed."

"Yeah."

"Well, thanks," Jacob said. He started to walk away.

Antonovich called him back. "Hey," he said softly. "You get that son of a bitch. You get whoever killed Josef. He was all right. Yes, he sold drugs, he sold arms, he sold...women. But he was an okay guy, you know?"

"Sure," Jacob said quietly. He didn't agree that Smirnoff was "an okay guy," but he did believe that a murderer should be brought to justice. Antonovich seemed passionate about catching Smirnoff's killer.

"You're going to the funeral?" Antonovich asked.

"Yes, of course."

"I want to go over to the cemetery. It's old—

and pretty big. Angels and archangels…and small mausoleums and large mausoleums."

"Places for a shooter to hide?" Jacob asked.

Antonovich nodded grimly. "I'll be checking it out," he said.

"Good. And good to know."

Jacob turned away. He knew the cemetery, on Eighth Street, or Calle Ocho, in the city. It was a beautiful cemetery. Gothic archways, handsome landscaping…and dozens of places for a shooter to hide—if Kozak was next in line, and there was still someone making a power play.

Antonovich appeared to be bitter about Smirnoff's death, as eager as any to pinpoint a killer. But Jacob just couldn't be sure what he felt he'd learned.

Either the goons were just hired muscle… or they had put together a trio of stone-cold killers, just waiting for the right moment to sweep in.

Which would mean that Victor Kozak was scheduled to die, as well.

Chapter Nine

Jorge left Jasmine's apartment at about 4:00 p.m. "I don't think I'm supposed to be hanging around here forever," he told her. "Despite the amount of fun and entertainment you're providing me, I've just got to go."

"What are you going to do?" Jasmine asked.

He smiled. "Hole up in my room with computer files. I'd rather hang around the beach. Check out the scene, hear what I can hear. But I guess that will be nothing. Rats. Guess I'll be hanging out with my computer."

"You don't think that's dangerous?"

"No, Bernie in tech helped me out. I hit a key, and only a genius could find my erased history or files or anything. I'll be okay. You'll be with a hot guy—I won't." He grinned at her.

She didn't grin back.

He walked over to her and hugged her.

"Partner, I can feel it. Mary is going to be okay. And you're going to be okay, and I'm going to be okay. Okay? Oh, and pretty man is going to be okay, too."

That one, at last, made her grin. "I'm sure. Fine, go work. And I'll—"

"Keep pacing."

"Yep, I'll keep pacing."

Jorge was gone; she was alone.

She found herself pondering Jacob Wolff. He seemed to know everything about her. Of course, he was with the federal government. She was MDPD—not any lesser, but still, a total difference in privileges and responsibilities. She was, however, sure that if the operation had been planned differently, she'd know much more about him. She didn't even know anything about the fake man, much less the real Jacob Wolff. She was probably lucky she knew his real name.

He probably even knew that her parents were working with a charity rebuilding houses down in Haiti.

She was working up a fair amount of aggravation by the time Jacob Wolff arrived at her apartment; she didn't notice at first that he seemed worn and weary when he walked in.

"Anything? Do you have anything at all?" she asked. "I believe that Connor will be with Kari again tonight—and I'm very afraid for what will happen to her after that."

"We've got field agents watching Connor. They can find nothing to suggest that he's a murderer."

"Oh, really? So, in your usual line of work, people advertise the fact that they're murderers?"

The way he looked at her, she wished she could swallow the words back.

"I don't know anything yet. I have a firm belief that the men just found in the Glades were the killers. I believe they worked for someone who copied the key to the balcony, and they didn't bother to escape that way—they just blended with a panicked crowd that was trampling one another. I actually don't believe Kozak called the shots, but I can't be sure. What have you got?"

"Why do you believe Kozak is innocent—of murder, that is?"

Jacob was looking straight ahead, at the television. "I think he would do a great deal to make money, but I think he's seen enough of death."

"What makes you believe that?"

He turned to look at her. "He has a past very much like my own. My father was born in Israel to parents who barely escaped the Nazis. My maternal grandfather made it out of one of Stalin's purges. I was lucky. I was born here. Almost right here—Mount Sanai. But my parents had to work hard. We were always just scraping by. We were here several years, and then in New York. I went to high school in Manhattan, and on to Columbia University with tuition assistance through the military— and then after my service, the FBI. I've been under the direction of great men with the Bureau for years, always FBI, but recently, FBI in conjunction with Homeland Security—and I've seen what's really, really ugly. So, I allow myself to be wrong. But I talk to people. I try to hear what's beneath what they say. I'm not perfect. I have been fooled now and then, but not often."

"So, you're the only one with a tough past, huh?"

He didn't reply. He looked away. "We'll need a place to go to dinner. We're definitely being watched, and while I'm not worried about our three stooges—who aren't all that stupid, I don't think—we're being watched by someone else, as well. I'm itching to get to the cemetery, but I know I have to trust others. I've called ahead. Miami field agents will be in the cemetery, in the mausoleums, around every angel high enough to cover a man. So, for us, for now..."

She sat next to him. He looked over at her.

She hesitated and then said, "I'm sorry. My past was a piece of cake. My parents are as sweet and kind as a pair of over overgrown lovebirds. I wanted to be a cop because my dad was a cop, and he was influential in catching a serial rapist at work on Eighth Street near Westchester. He somehow managed to teach us about the evils of the world and see the beauty in it, as well. He never whined about me becoming a cop because I was a woman, and neither did my mother. I never wanted for anything. I was helped through college. I... I'm sorry."

He reached across the sofa and took her hand. And they weren't playacting for anyone, because no one was in the room.

"I know," he told her. He grinned. "I've seen your file."

"And I haven't seen yours. I don't even know… Are you married?"

"I was."

"Divorced?"

"No."

"Oh. I'm…sorry."

"It's been a long time," he said.

"Still."

He shrugged and smiled. "You would have liked her."

"I'm sure I would have," she said softly.

He was studying her, to a point where she flushed. "What?"

"I'm a classic case—that's what an analyst would say, I'm pretty sure. Married young, the sweet love of youth, lost that love, plowed into work, kind of a loner. Way too much time undercover for serious relationships…"

She was definitely blushing by then.

"So I've read your file, but there's nothing in there that explains the you that Jorge knows—and told me all about."

"I'm going to kill him."

"Don't. He's your partner. And he loves you."

"Okay, so I don't have a haunted history.

And I didn't lose anyone. I mean, I didn't lose a husband or a lover. I just…"

"Well, if you don't go out, you don't meet anyone."

"Seriously, I'm going to kill Jorge."

He grinned. "I really like Jorge. So?"

"Okay, I don't often work undercover. But I do work major crimes. And even though you have shifts with other officers and you work with other agencies, there are times you have to be dedicated to the case instead of getting to know the people you're working with. When you're the one a loved one of a victim is depending on, or you're the one who's gained the trust of a young witness, or…"

Her voice trailed. His elbow was angled on the couch and he was smiling as he watched her.

"Many men find female police detectives to be intimidating," she went on. "And many of those who don't are a little scary themselves. It's not that I don't go out, or I don't believe in going out—"

"Just haven't found the right guy?"

She shrugged, rising nervously. She hadn't expected the evening to turn into a tell-all, especially when she sure as hell couldn't tell the truth about her feelings regarding him.

She walked over to the door. "I guess we'd better go to dinner. Let's see…where haven't we been?"

He stood and met her at the entry. "I don't know. Where do you suggest?" They were facing each other, ridiculously close.

And then, they both heard a shuffling sound, just outside.

"Someone following you?" she mouthed to Jacob.

He carefully looked out. "Maybe," he mouthed back. He drew his gun. He checked the door, and she saw that he had double-bolted it.

To her surprise, he threw the door open.

Night was falling. But the way the apartment building had been laid out, the pool and patio area faced the west, and while the night encroached, the lowering sun created a sky of bold beauty. Soon, the radiant colors would be gone, and it would be the darkness that reigned.

"Ah, what a lovely night. Maybe later…" Jacob said, his voice carrying. And then, still speaking with a full rich voice, he turned to her. "On second thought, why don't we order in tonight?" he asked.

Was there someone out there? A figure, to the side in the shadows, hunkered down in a lawn chair?

The door was fully open. They were on display, and he was looking down at her with his brilliant blue eyes, so handsome and so startling against his dark hair and bronzed face.

Jacob pulled her into his arms and kissed her. And this time, he pulled her close. His mouth came down on hers while his arms encompassed her, his hands sliding down low against her back, drawing her ever closer, his tongue parting her lips and slipping deep within her mouth.

The door slowly closed behind them while they backed inside the apartment, locked in the passionate embrace.

He was still kissing her as he eased one hand away, once again double-bolting the lock. She heard the sound as the bolts slid into place. And only then did his hold ease, his lips part from hers.

They were still so close. He looked down at her, and she could still feel the dampness of her lips, burning as they seemed to do when he touched her.

"I think…" she murmured, and he leaned closer, as if to hear her. His lips were almost upon hers again, his body was all but touching hers. To her amazement, she almost smiled, and she said softly, "Oh, screw this!"

She moved back into his arms. She was tall, but she moved up on tiptoe, the length of her body against his. She moved her mouth that one inch closer, found his lips and kissed him, parting his mouth, delving deep within it with her tongue, initiating all. She was stunned by her own movements, but more so by the depth of the longing and desire that was sweeping through her.

The kiss deepened and deepened. She pressed closer to him, flush against him, and felt his hands travel down the length of her body. The kiss broke, and he eased back slightly.

She felt she was panting like an idiot, and he had moved away. A flush of heat broke over her, and her limbs began to tremble. She had to force herself to bring her eyes to his, but when she did, she saw he was still watching her, intensely alert. He smiled slightly and said,

"Ummmm." He was still holding her, and then he arched a brow and whispered, "Oh, screw this."

He swept her up, higher, into his arms. His mouth found hers again, but he moved as he kissed her, across the floor, toward the apartment bedroom. In seconds, they were lying down together on the bed. He braced himself over her, and said softly, "Only if it's what you really want."

She smiled. His pausing to question her, to be very sure, added to her sense of attraction and desperation.

She reached out, drawing his face down to hers again. She replied with her hands on his face, caressing his face as she drew him to her. "Yes. So much." They kissed again…just kissed, and then he straddled above her, doffing his jacket. The Glock he carried was evident then, and he reached back for the gun and holster, leaning over to set them on the dresser.

He looked down at her a moment.

"Mine's inside the bedside drawer, to the left," she told him. Now they both knew where to reach if they were threatened in any way at any time.

That solved, he struggled from his shirt; she

rose up to help him. He was still in trousers, socks and shoes. He halfway rolled from her, divesting his clothing, and she slipped out of the cool knit dress she'd been wearing, as well as her bra and panties.

To her surprise, he suddenly made an urgent sound, almost like a growl, rising to meet her again.

Naked flesh against naked flesh, he whispered, "So wrong of me. I knew the moment I saw you on the runway that you were extraordinary, you were grace and laughter and beauty, and I wanted you, but I didn't know what it would mean when I knew you…"

When his mouth found hers again, she felt the burn that had teased her lips become something of a raging wildfire that snaked down the length of her body. She allowed herself to roam free with her hands, loving the curve of his shoulders, the clench of muscle in his shoulders and down his back. She felt his body harden against her own, and she couldn't wrap herself tightly enough to him, to be both almost in his skin and touch him just the same.

They fell back on the bed together and she lay on top of him, landing kisses on his neck and his shoulders, the hard planes of his stomach, and moving lower against his body.

His hands grabbed her back, and they flipped in the bed. His mouth fell upon her throat and her breasts and lingered and teased and caressed. Those kisses continued downward, and she arched and writhed against him, finding his flesh and returning each touch of passion and hunger and longing.

She thought she would burn to a cinder, she was so alive, burning with a need unlike anything she'd ever known, wanting the play to go on forever, yet desperate that something be touched, that he be within her, as well.

And then he was, and they were moving, and moving, and moving...

They rolled, their lips melded together again and the rock of his hips was incredible. The sense of him within her was almost more than she could bear, the absolute sweetness, the rise of that fire, that longing to be ever more a part of him. Rising...and bursting out upon her like a flow of liquid gold.

The night seemed to sweep in all around her for long moments as she felt little bits of ecstasy shoot through her, ebbing bit by incredible bit, until she felt the damp sheen of their flesh, still so taut together, the rise and fall of her breath, the rock-hard pounding of her heart. And him, still holding her, still clinging in the darkness to the awesome beauty of what had been. So real, flesh and blood and pulse and their gasps for air...

They didn't speak at first; they just breathed.

And then he whispered softly, "I don't think I'll be putting that in the report."

She smiled and turned to him. "I understand you're often by the book. Forgive me."

"Forgive you?" He straddled her again, catching her hands and leaning low, his eyes alight with humor and tenderness. "Ah, my dear Detective Adair. It is I who must ask forgiveness. On second thought, no. Can't ask forgiveness. This was—"

"Incredible," she whispered.

"More than incredible. I don't know the words... Maybe there are none."

She pulled him back to her, and the kiss they shared was sweet and tender, and still, she knew, could arouse again at any second.

He pulled away and got out of bed suddenly. Light from the living room swept into the bedroom and she could see the full leanly muscled perfection of his tightly honed body in the doorway. He wasn't self-conscious as he padded out to the living room. Curious, she rose up on an arm.

Then he was back, every movement sleek and fluid, and he fell down beside her again. "Checking the door," he murmured.

"There's still someone out there?" she asked.

"Sitting by the pool. We'll order in," he told her.

He moved toward her and she jumped back suddenly, stricken. She'd been so enraptured with the man she'd been lucky enough to come to know that she had all but forgotten this wasn't an ordinary job.

She was looking for Mary. And even though Mary still seemed beyond her reach...

"Kari!" she exclaimed. "I'm worried, Jacob. What about Kari—and Mr. Connor?"

"I'll call in," he assured her. He found his jacket where he'd flung it earlier and dug his phone out of the pocket. After a minute, he had the info.

"Kari is back at her apartment."

"She's all right? And they're back inside?"

"Just Kari is back at her place. Connor took her out for a steak dinner and then a moonlit stroll on the beach. Then he brought her home. He left shortly, a smile on his face."

"Oh," Jasmine said. "Jacob, you don't think she'll be in any trouble with the gang for…for not sleeping with him?"

"No, I don't think she'll be in trouble."

Jasmine was still unsure. "He's being watched, Jasmine. Kari will be okay. Someone will get to Connor soon enough."

"Kari was worried though. I think she felt something was off. And I can't forget about Mary…"

"We'll find Mary. I swear it," he told her.

She believed him. And miraculously, she could move forward with her own night, grateful that the young blonde woman was all right. For now.

And there was nothing they could do. Not for the night.

She moved forward, catching his face, looking up into the dazzling blue of his eyes. "Thank you."

He kissed her again, that tender kiss… But the kiss deepened, and then it began to travel, and he was kissing her breasts again, affording each the most tender caresses, and her belly and thighs, bringing that erotic fire with every touch.

She let the night seize her again, and she returned his caresses, unable to stop seeking more and more of him, know the taste of his skin, the taste of him.

They embraced tightly, and he was within her, and they rolled, and she was atop him, and this time they laughed and teased and whispered.

And then they lay together again, just breathing, still afrire, savoring the beauty of the darkness of the night, the coolness of the sheets beneath their bodies.

She was the one to sit up and straddle him this time.

He smiled, catching her hands with his. "Leave it to a cop to always want to be on top." He rolled her over, covering her with his body.

"And leave it to a Fed to think he must be in control."

"This Fed," he said softly, "is just happy to be with you."

She smiled back at him, wishing that the night would never end; that this was all they needed in reality and that the world would go away.

It could not.

He rolled from her, standing. "Food—we need to order food."

"I am hungry," she agreed.

She leaped out of bed, reaching to the foot of it for the caftan robe she kept there. He found his boxers but bothered with nothing else. He was already out in the living room, his phone drawn from his pocket. He looked at her. "I have a delivery service so, Chinese, Indian, Italian... Steaks? Seafood? What's your pleasure?"

You are my pleasure! she thought.

She managed not to say it out loud. "I'm easy. Food-wise," she added quickly. "Anything."

"Wow. I found one with pizza and champagne. Now there's an interesting combo. But I don't think that champagne... Not tonight."

"Not tonight," she agreed.

It was one thing to be drunk on desire when you were supposed to be drunk on desire. But quite another to have anything that might alter the mind with a goon outside on the porch.

"I don't believe we're in any danger, but I've seen things change quickly," he told her. "Ah, Thai food!"

"Perfect."

She stood near him and looked over his shoulder as he went through the offerings. They decided on one noodle dish and one rice dish.

Jasmine suddenly felt extremely awkward.

"Coffee!" she said. "I should make some coffee."

She started to walk into the kitchen. He caught her arm and pulled her back to him, holding her there, looking into her eyes. "Please, don't go away from me," he said softly.

She knew he didn't mean she shouldn't go into the kitchen and make coffee.

"I...it sounds like a line," she told him, "but I've never...in my life...just done this so quickly... I guess I don't know how to act."

"And I hope you believe me. I've always drawn a line. Until tonight."

She stood on her toes and kissed his lips lightly. "I won't go away," she promised.

She made coffee; Thai food arrived. Jacob made a point of answering the door still clad just in his boxers. He was careful to double-bolt the door again, and then to bring his Glock back out to sit on the table while they ate.

"You know, I'm a damned good markswoman," she told him.

He smiled at her. "I'd expect no less." He picked at a strand of the noodles. "Oh, by the way, Kozak gave you to me today." His smiled deepened as he saw her stiffen. "Sorry. All in a role."

She hesitated. "But in truth, I give myself where I choose."

"And so do I," he told her.

She laughed softly. Much of the Thai food went uneaten; they wound up laughing over a noodle they had both chosen.

And then they wound up in one another's arms again.

THERE WAS A knock on the door.

Jacob rolled out of bed, instantly awake. He grabbed his trousers and then his gun. Jasmine followed him out of bed in a flash, slipping on a robe, going for her own weapon.

He took a quick glance at the clock on the nightstand: 9:00 a.m. He headed out of the bedroom quickly, with Jasmine on his heels.

But one look out the peephole had Jacob unlocking the door. "It's all right. A friend," he told her.

Jorge stepped in, looked at both of them and then smiled.

"Method acting!" he said. "I like it. Just wondering what the hell took you two so long."

Chapter Ten

The funeral service was long. Speaking in Russian, the priest delivered the service with all respect and care—while the man might have known about Smirnoff and his deeds, he didn't judge when it came time for a man to meet his Maker. It was actually beautiful, though Jacob was sure many in the congregation had no idea what was being said.

Victor Kozak gave an emotional speech about his friend, and he did so in English for the benefit of the mourners who had gathered.

Many had come out to pay their respects—not so many would be invited to the celebration of life that would come later, at the club. Equally, not so many would travel with the funeral train that would follow the hearse to the cemetery.

Jacob had spoken with his Miami counterpart, Dean Jenkins. He knew agents were already waiting at the cemetery.

It would be a fine day for an attempt on Victor Kozak's life.

Jenkins also filled him in on what was happening with events at the morgue, and with the local crime scene technicians.

"They identified one of the dead men, from the hand they got out of the alligator's gullet. Ain't technology great? Although, to be honest, it wasn't fingerprints or anything like that. One of my guys working in Little Havana recognized the ring.

"The victim was Leonardo Gonzalez—an undocumented Venezuelan immigrant. He and a few of his fellows had traveled through Mexico and, according to our agent, onto a cruise ship and into Miami. He'd been a contract killer at home and was looking for work in Little Havana. He was happy to work for anyone but was looking for connections in the Little Havana area because he didn't speak any English.

"Anyway…according to our sources, he was the kind of really bad guy taking serious advantage of the criminal activity going on down there right now, but he might have crossed another crime lord, meaning it was time for him to get out. But he had his own little gang. I'm working under the assumption our other two headless bodies are associates of his."

"Thanks— Anything new on Donald McPherson Connor?"

"We followed him. He was a perfect gentleman with the young lady. And he left her at her door. An agent is still outside. He could have followed Connor, or he could have kept his eye on her. He chose to protect the one we know to be an innocent. Anyway, we have a new crew out on the streets today. Oh, they're checking in at your art gallery, too, making sure that Special Agent Partridge is doing okay."

"Thanks. Hey, should I be getting a new phone?"

"Not to worry, I'm listed as a local artist. You any closer?" Jenkins asked him.

"I don't know. I'm going to see what happens at the funeral."

They ended their call, and Jacob joined the mourners, making himself one with Ivan Petrov and the three goons.

Jasmine was not invited to this part of the day; she would be at the club, preparing to work with the food and drinks that would be served. He tried not to worry. He knew she was an accomplished policewoman, and he believed she was an excellent markswoman. She was also vulnerable, though he had warned her that she should be wary at all times—and armed if any way possible.

She knew that, of course.

Kozak hadn't asked Jacob to drive to the cemetery; he wanted him next to him in his car, behind the driver, who would be Antonovich.

Jacob couldn't help but wonder if Kozak was afraid that Antonovich could shoot them both if Jacob was driving—he'd be easy prey for a man sitting behind him.

They arrived safely at the cemetery. It was just west of the downtown area known as Calle Ocho. The cemetery had recently joined with two different companies that had been offering funeral arrangements and grave sites since the 1850s back in Cuba. It was at the edge of a neighborhood close to downtown known as Little Havana.

But like most of Miami, anyone and everyone might be here.

They entered through Gothic arches. The grounds were sweeping, well tended and beautiful. Trees cast shady spots everywhere, and the park stretched for long blocks. They drove around a winding trail until they reached the canopy that stood over the area where the body of Josef Smirnoff would be laid to rest.

The cars parked; Jacob got out and waited for Kozak to emerge from the car, as well. He looked around. A lovely marble angel stood guard over a nearby family lot; a small family mausoleum stood about fifty yards away. Another, about a hundred yards farther out.

They were under a gracious old oak, near to a grouping of military headstones. Down a bit farther was a large concrete memorial to a man who had been a Mason and with the Mahi Shrine. His memorial gave witness to the fact that he had spent forty years as a Shriner, dedicating his time to raising funds for the children's hospital.

Probably a great guy. Right now, Jacob had to be certain that his memorial wasn't hiding a sniper.

He continued his scan of the area. The large mausoleum with its beautiful stained-glass windows, known to house many, many bodies, was perhaps a hundred yards behind them. A great place for a sniper to hide.

He reminded himself that the Miami agents knew this cemetery, where to be and where to watch.

And still he was on high alert.

"There, Mr. Kozak," Antonovich said, coming around to Kozak's side. "The chairs in front, sir. Those are for you and those who were close to Josef."

Sticking to Kozak's side like a piece of lint, Jacob led the man to the chairs.

Josef Smirnoff might not have been a cold-blooded killer, but he sure as hell had been a criminal. Victor Kozak had taken over from him, and while he might not be a cold-blooded killer either, he was also a major criminal.

But the showing of respectable people at the cemetery was large enough; the local news media brought trucks to the winding road that led through the very large cemetery—another place for a shooter to hide. Politicians and other respectable citizens arrived to say goodbye to Smirnoff.

Jacob sat back as the priest gave the grave-side prayers. He had to have faith in his fellow agents. But just as he had settled—still alert and ready—a latecomer arrived at the grave site.

It was the man who so disturbed Jasmine. Donald McPherson Connor.

THE CLUB WAS a bustle of activity when Jasmine arrived, even though it was early. The catering company personnel included two chefs, two wine stewards and six members of a cleanup crew.

Jasmine and Jorge reported right away to the dressing room. The servers were suited out appropriately—men in tuxes, women in similar versions with short skirts instead of pants—and shown the various food stations and the additional bars.

"Remember, today, you serve quickly, politely and quietly. We honor Josef," Natasha instructed. "You all understand? Behavior is beyond circumspect."

Stopping by one of the makeup tables where Jasmine had just harnessed her own hair in a braid at the back of her neck, Jorge told her, "Five City of Miami Beach cops, all aware to watch for trouble—hired on by Kozak." He lowered his head to her, pretending to smooth back a piece of her hair. "The chef at the first table is a plant—FBI. We have representation from MDPD as well—Detective Birch. You've worked with her. She'll be on the arm of one of our young politicians."

"Sounds good," Jasmine murmured. "Then again, how many cops were prowling the show when Josef was killed?"

"There's a cop at the balcony door. If anyone is going to start shooting, it won't be from the balcony." He leaned closer still, pretending to flick a piece of nonexistent lint from her brow. "FBI is crawling over the cemetery, too. Thing is, the killer must know. Unless he—or she—is really an egotistical bastard, nothing will happen today."

Nothing would happen. This would go on…

Jorge grinned suddenly. "You look different."

"I don't dress this way often."

"No, it's the way your eyes are shining."

"Jorge."

"It's nice to see you happy."

She looked at him and then lowered her head, ruefully smiling. "I'd like to see you happy."

"Hey, you may. I'm not watched, not the way you are," he told her. "I had some dinner out last night. Sat on the beach."

"Jorge, you have to be—"

"I was careful. Trust me."

He grinned, and she knew it was the truth.

"Jorge, I need you!" Natasha called. "Now, you will take the large silver tray—you have nice long arms. Move through the crowd but offer up the food. Do not interfere with people who are talking. You let them stop. Think of yourselves as courteous machines."

Jorge moved on. Jasmine saw Kari at the next dressing table and she stood, heading over to her.

"Need help with anything?" she asked.

"Nope," Kari said, looking up. "I never can do false eyelashes right, but Natasha says we shouldn't wear them today."

"They're miserable things anyway."

"I agree."

"So, how are you?" Jasmine asked her softly.

"Good. Great, really."

"Great?" Jasmine asked.

Kari smiled. "I know that he's old, but honestly, if I were, say, forty-five instead of twenty-two, well... He has such a great accent. He talked to me about books and plays and he told me so much history about this place that I didn't know... He's kind, Jasmine. So very kind."

"Great to hear. I thought he made you a bit nervous. Are you okay with him now? When do you see him again?"

"Tonight. Later, of course. I told him—and I'm sure Natasha told him—that the club models were working the funeral, and we wouldn't be available until the entire celebration of life came to an end. He told me that, no matter what the hour, he'd like to see me." Kari hesitated a moment and then whispered, "I don't know why I was worried. Jasmine, we had the best dinner. Such a lovely night. He's truly so well educated. And then I thought he would want more. I thought he would want me to sleep with him. Oh! And he talked about Mary. He said she was such a lovely person—he was sure she went on to resume her education. They had talked about school and always having a backup to modeling or acting. He believes she might have headed out to California."

California? Or the pit of an alligator's stomach, somewhere out in the Everglades.

"I guess he's worked with or been a client of these people for a while," Jasmine said.

"Not so long. He told me that the group here—well, Josef Smirnoff first, and now Victor Kozak—knew how to find the most cultured women. He likes to go to the theater and the opera and art shows, and…he needs the right escorts."

"How nice."

"He loves music and musicals, voices!"

The opera…or screams as a woman died beneath a knife?

"Jasmine, he's really such a gentleman. I thought he might be the type to immediately demand that we sleep together, that…"

"What?"

"That he might want me to do weird things." Her voice dropped to a whisper. "You know, weird sexual things. Scary things." She swallowed. "You know…autoerotic asphyxiation, or maybe not even scary things, just disgusting things. But he didn't even press sleeping with me." She paused, seeming a little uncomfortable, then went on quietly. "We're not specifically *ordered* to sleep with the clients, but there's an understanding that they get what they want if they're paying the price. And that trickles down to us in money and…in prestige on the runway. It's no secret that Natasha's highest earners get the best gigs. But… this guy, no pressure. I'm babbling. I guess I am still maybe a little nervous."

"Kari, you have my number, right? If not, I'll make sure that you do now."

Kari pulled out her phone and Jasmine quickly gave her the number to her burner phone.

"We're having lunch, right?" Kari asked.

"Lunch, yes, but keep your phone near. If you're afraid at any point, you call me immediately!"

Kari frowned, but then smiled. "You can call me, too, you know, except that… Well! You seem just fine, and I imagine…" She broke off and laughed suddenly, leaning forward. "I might have been willing to pay some big bucks myself for that blue-eyed wonder who chose you."

Jasmine smiled weakly.

"You're okay, right?" Kari asked. "I mean, with him."

"Yes, I'm just fine," Jasmine managed.

"What is he like, that Jacob? Those eyes of his… If he ever looked at me the way he looks at you, wow. I'd be putty."

"Putty," Jasmine repeated. "That's me."

"Girls!" Natasha called. "Time to take your stations. Sasha has called—the services at the grave site are ending. We will be ready, the most gracious of hosts and hostesses."

And so, they were on. They all trailed out of the dressing room.

Natasha was by the balcony door; it was open for them to head down the stairs.

Jasmine smiled as she passed Natasha. Only Kozak was supposed to have a key. But Victor wasn't here. And Ivan was downstairs, setting up the main bar, giving orders to the catering company.

Jasmine hurried downstairs along with the others. She knew that somehow, she would get that information to Jacob.

Lightning didn't strike twice…

Unless sometimes, it did.

NO BULLETS RANG out at the cemetery.

The priest, resplendent in his robes, carried through the service. Women had been given roses; they walked past the coffin to drop them down upon it.

"I need a moment," Kozak told his companions.

He was at the coffin alone, except for the four cemetery workers who waited discreetly to see that the coffin was lowered six feet under. The hearse was preparing to leave. Antonovich, Suarez and Garibaldi waited while other mourners filed out to their cars.

Donald McPherson Connor was starting to walk away.

Jacob was a distance from Victor Kozak as it was; he wouldn't be any farther from the man if he walked toward Connor. He excused himself to the trio of bodyguards.

"Mr. Connor!" Jacob called out.

The man stopped walking and looked back at him, eyeing him distastefully. Jacob noticed that he was lean but fit.

Probably plenty strong. Certainly strong enough against a slim blonde girl.

Connor was evidently irritated at having been stopped—by Jacob, at any rate. "Yes, Mr. Marensky, what is it?"

"Well, I just wish to apologize, and I hope that we don't keep bad blood between us. I was, in fact, hoping that you found Miss Anderson to be up to your expectations."

"Miss Anderson is a truly lovely woman. I am enjoying her company."

Jacob forced a smile. "Excellent. She is quite beautiful."

"Not as intriguing as Miss Alamein though,"

Connor said. He was an oddly dignified man—soft-spoken. "So, Mr. Marenksy, what exactly do you do in relation to the Gold Sun Club?"

Then again, Jacob had seen some of the most innocent and soft-spoken men and women possible turn out to be vicious and as cold as ice.

"We have shared business interests. I run an art gallery," Jacob said.

"So I hear," Connor said, his British accent a little clipped.

"I'd welcome you for a visit. See if there's anything that catches your eye. Just what is your enterprise, sir?"

The man's smile tightened. "No enterprise—other than the stock market. Now there, sir, is bloody criminal action from the get-go, and yet quite legal."

"Ah, I believed that you had worked with Josef—and now Victor."

"I simply require a certain kind of companion."

"I see," Jacob said, still smiling. Just what was it that he required? "Well, sir, I shall see you at the club. I just wished to clear the air between us. Please understand, my arrangements had been made first."

"Oh, yes, I understand perfectly, Mr. Marensky." Connor was still looking at him with watery blue hatred.

"Jacob?" Kozak was calling to him.

"Excuse me," Jacob said, spinning around to return to Victor Kozak's side.

"We must be leaving now," Kozak said.

"Yes, of course."

"You and Connor are good then?" Kozak asked him softly.

"Oh, as good as we can be, Victor. As good as we can be."

"Please, then…" Kozak indicated the road through the cemetery; theirs was the only car that remained. "Sasha, you will drive."

"Yes, sir," Antonovich said, sliding into the driver's seat.

Garibaldi took the front seat by him. Kozak slid into the back, between Suarez and Jacob. The car rolled out of the cemetery, onto Southwest Eighth Street and then headed for I-95 and the extension out to South Beach.

The funeral itself had gone off without a hitch. Now, all they had to do was make it through the reception—the celebration of life where the mourners would come together and Smirnoff would receive his last honors.

Smirnoff, Kozak and their peers really were

criminals. Jacob had seen one too many a decent person cajoled into and then hooked on drugs. And abusing the trust of hopeful girls was reprehensible. But Jacob wanted Kozak prosecuted and locked away—not on a slab with a bullet in his head.

As the car rolled up to Kozak's special parking place at the back of the property, Jacob felt Kozak's hand wind into a vice on his arm.

The man looked at him, and there was fear in his eyes, quickly masked as Garibaldi came around and opened the door.

Jacob got out.

"My friend, I know you will change things!" Kozak said. He caught Jacob's arm again, turning to show him where they were. "Cops— down there, at the end of the block. That guy with the long hair and the beggar's cup at this end? A cop." He pulled Jacob along to show him the men to whom he was referring.

And then he whispered to Jacob, "Here. This is where they will try to kill me. Somewhere here, at the club."

Chapter Eleven

It always amazed Jasmine to see the people who came out for such an event—the last rites for a man they had to have known conducted criminal activities. She was also certain many people on the guest list had not sat through the long religious ceremony at the church, nor attended the final graveside services.

The club was busy within minutes of the door opening.

Ivan stood at the main doors dressed in his best designer suit. Natasha was at his side tonight, ready to greet everyone as they came in; she had finished her busywork, prepared her various crews and was ready to be the grand hostess.

Jasmine had been given a tray of canapés to carry around, and she did so smoothly and easily. Though maintaining her demeanor as a courteous robot was not as easy as it might have been—Kozak and the goons and Jacob had yet to come into the club.

When they finally did, she breathed an inward sigh of relief.

She tried to maneuver herself around to Jacob's position casually, making it part of her regular sweep of the room. When she made it to an area near the street entrance, he was still standing with Kozak and the bodyguards.

"Gentlemen," she said quietly, offering up her tray.

The bodyguards quickly reached for the little quiches. Jacob inclined his head slightly and took a canapé, as well.

Kozak turned to her. "What I need is a drink, Jasmine. Will you get me a vodka? I'm sure that Natasha has seen to it that our hired bartender knows what is my special reserve."

"Yes, of course," Jasmine said.

But Natasha swept by at that moment, giving her a serious frown. "Jasmine, you are to move among our guests."

"Yes, Natasha," she said.

"Natasha," Kozak said softly. "We have many people working the floor. I would like Jasmine to go and get me my drink."

"Victor, I can do that for you," Natasha said.

"You are the hostess. Let Jasmine go," Kozak said. "It's time that I...that I welcome our guests and give my little speech here, eh? But one vodka first!"

Jasmine headed off to the bar. The man there gave her an appreciative look and she smiled in return. "I need a drink for Mr. Kozak—his special reserve. He believes you'll know what it is."

"Yep," the bartender said. "I've been given the bottle and serious instructions. It's a unique vintage from Russia, not sold in the United States." He grinned at her, reaching beneath the bar for the bottle. He got a glass and said, "Just two ice cubes. Rich men and their drinks."

"Thanks," she told him.

"I live to serve. Come see me again!"

She nodded and started to hurry away but turned back. "Did you meet with Mr. Kozak before this event? Did he give you the bottle?" she asked.

He shook his head. "I met with the praying mantis. Oh, sorry—the entire catering company met with Natasha. She gave us strict instructions."

"And the bottle of vodka?"

"No, it was here where she said it would be when I came in. Hey, sorry, I hope she's not a friend of yours—I'm an actor and this catering company keeps me in cash while I'm pounding the pavement. I'm sorry. Please, I didn't mean to be offensive."

"You need to be a lot more careful."

"Please, don't get me fired."

"I won't, but... Never mind. Thank you."

Once again, she turned away, but then something about the situation seemed disturbing. "Would you mind? Give me four more drinks, just like this one but with regular vodka. Something good, just not Kozak's special reserve."

"Anything for you."

She smiled. And prayed that she and Jacob had come to know one another in their undercover roles as well as they had come to know one another personally.

Kozak and Jacob, with Garibaldi, Suarez, and Antonovich behind them, were heading toward the stage. Jasmine took a step back, her heart pounding, wondering if she was wrong and if she might just cause the entire operation to implode—and put them all, including the guests, in serious danger.

But her hunch was strong. She had seen Natasha with the key.

Natasha was definitely sleeping with Kozak—but had she been sleeping with Josef Smirnoff before? Was she part of what came with taking over the business because she wouldn't be ousted herself?

Jasmine walked toward the men.

"Special for Mr. Kozak, and gentlemen, I believe it was a long day for you, as well. I hope I have not displeased you, Mr. Kozak."

She looked at Jacob, just lowering her eyes at the glass he was to take, and gave the barest shake of her head. He shouldn't drink it. He would know—surely, he would know!

Jacob's striking blue eyes fell on hers. Before Kozak could answer, he said, "That was very thoughtful of you."

"Nice, sweet, as always," Antonovich said happily, and he looked at Kozak.

"Definitely. One vodka, boss, eh?" Suarez asked.

"One vodka," Kozak agreed.

Jasmine dared look around as the men took their drinks. An up-and-coming beach politician was entering with a lovely young news reporter on his arm. Natasha was doing her duty and greeting them.

"I must get to the stage," Kozak said.

"I'll get you there swiftly," Jacob assured him.

Jasmine flashed a smile to all of them. "I'd best get to my canapés," she said. She started to walk away.

"A second?" Jacob asked, looking at Kozak for permission, as well.

"Yes, then you will walk with me, stand by me, at my back," Kozak said.

Jacob smiled and stepped away with Jasmine. She had her chance. "Natasha had the key tonight," she said. "Might be important. Kozak wasn't here. I don't think they plan a shooting."

"Poison in the vodka?"

"I could be wrong."

"Thanks. You gave it to me."

"You knew!"

"I knew," he assured her, and then he squeezed her hand and stepped back.

"To the stage," Kozak said. He seemed very nervous.

As he should be! Jasmine thought.

As he walked away, Kozak took a sip of

his vodka. He frowned instantly. The man did know the taste of his special reserve.

And that wasn't his special reserve.

But Jacob guided him toward the stage. Jasmine saw Jacob casually and discreetly set his own glass down on a waiter's tray.

The waiter was Jorge. He looked across the room at her and nodded.

JACOB STOOD JUST behind Victor Kozak as the man took the microphone, thanking everyone for coming, and for honoring Josef Smirnoff. He told a few tales about his friend and talked about the way Smirnoff had loved Miami Beach and how the club had been a dream for him.

"Sparkling like the Miami sun!" Victor said. "He was my business partner. He was my friend. In his honor, we will rename the club—it will be *Josef's* when it opens to the public tomorrow night. While we faced senseless violence and his death here, we are a powerful people. We are South Floridians, whether we were born here or we were lucky enough to enter this country and find this paradise as our home. We are strong. And, in his name, we will prevail!"

As Kozak spoke, Jacob kept his eyes on the room. He also mused that Kozak didn't think that peddling escorts or drug dealing were really bad things to do. Illegal, but not bad.

He saw the police—in uniform, and undercover—and the agents in the room. And he knew each of them was watching for the first sign, so much as a hint, of the barrel of a gun or someone reaching into a pocket.

But he was pretty sure Jasmine was right; guns would not be blazing. A killer must right now be waiting for whatever poison might have been in the special reserve to work.

"Make it quick," Jacob managed to whisper.

Kozak took heed. He quickly asked the crowd to honor Smirnoff's memory and enjoy his dream. Then Jacob took his arm and led him from the stage.

"Tell your men you feel sick," he said. "That I'm going to get you upstairs."

Kozak heeded him once again. "I am unwell! Sasha, you will watch the east stairs. Antonio, you will watch the west. Alejandro, you will take between them. I am... I must sit down. Alone. The day... It has been too long. Mr. Marensky will see me upstairs to my office. Tell Ivan and Natasha they must remain the finest hosts."

"Yes, sir," Garibaldi said quickly.

"Hurry, and stumble as we walk up," Jacob said quietly to Kozak.

Antonovich nodded to the policeman at the base of the stairs; the man noticed Kozak, nodded in return and unlatched the velvet barrier. Jacob set his arm on Kozak's back and they headed up the stairs. Halfway up, Kozak pretended to stumble.

"Good, good, we keep going," Jacob murmured.

They passed the expected security. They made it to the door, and Jacob passed through it quickly. A cop met them in the hall.

"Getting Mr. Kozak to his office," Jacob told him.

The cop nodded.

They opened the door to the office—despite the massive security, Jacob entered first.

The office was empty. He had expected it would be. The killer would be waiting for Kozak to fall downstairs.

And everyone would think the day had been just too difficult for Victor Kozak. The man drank, he liked his cigars, and maybe he liked some of his smuggled product, too. His heart could just give out, after a day like today.

And the poison wouldn't be found during an autopsy, since such substances would not fall into the realm of regular tests.

Kozak sat behind his desk and sighed deeply. "I really could use a drink!"

"I'm sure you keep something in here. Then again, I'm sure there are others who know you keep something in here," Jacob warned him.

"So. I will not drink. What do I do?" Kozak asked.

"We wait here. We see if someone comes. Maybe we call an ambulance. We let the crowd know you're in the emergency room, barely hanging on."

Kozak drummed his fingers on his desk, smiling. He stared at Jacob.

"You are not an art dealer, are you, Mr. Marensky? As a matter of fact, your name isn't even Marensky, is it?"

THE NIGHT SEEMED VERY, very long.

Jasmine moved about the floor as she had been directed, watching the stairs now and then. She saw Jorge with one of the catering crew, an FBI plant, and knew the vodka was probably already on its way to be tested.

But the bartender, she was sure, had just been hired on for the night.

She saw the other girls milling about the room, doing exactly what they had been told to do. They were pretty and silent and moving like robots. She watched the stairs. And to her relief, people began to leave.

While the club had been open and music—soft, somber music, much of it Russian—had played through the night, there was no dancing. After the speech, after the food and free-flowing alcohol, there was little else to do.

People murmured about coming when the club was up and running again. Big names in music had been booked before Smirnoff's death—they were probably still on the agenda.

She was doing her last round with coffees and coffee liqueurs when she saw the man, Donald McPherson Connor, stop Kari Anderson and talk to her. Then he slipped out the door.

A moment later, Kari followed.

Jasmine walked back to the bar quickly, ready to dispose of her tray and head out.

But there was a man at the bar. A little man

with big glasses, a nerdy smile and wild bushy hair. "Don't," he said softly, then called to the bartender. "Another, my friend!"

"Pardon?" Jasmine asked, setting her tray down. She didn't care what he was saying; Jacob had Kozak upstairs. Things were coming to a head. And Kari was leaving with a man who just might be a very sick murderer.

"No, we're on it," the little man said. He spoke more loudly. "I mean, man, you're not just a beauty, lady, you are really cool looking. Those eyes of yours—emeralds!" He lowered his voice while pretending to study her eyes. "Special Agent Dean Jenkins, working in association with Wolff. We have a man following Connor and Miss Anderson. Keep your cover."

"That's very nice of you, sir," she said. "I work for the club. We don't date customers."

Garibaldi came up behind her. "Is there a problem?" he asked, glaring at the man who had just identified himself to her as FBI.

Dean Jenkins lifted his hands. "No, sir. No problem. I'm totally a hands-off guy, just complimenting beauty."

"He was very sweet. No problem at all," Jasmine said quickly.

To her relief, Garibaldi ambled away.

Jasmine turned with her tray of coffee cups and coffee drinks.

Natasha was standing there. "All is well?"

"Yes, of course."

"Have you seen Mr. Marensky?" Natasha asked her.

"I believe he went up with Mr. Kozak. He wasn't feeling well."

"They are upstairs? Still?"

Jasmine didn't have to answer. She heard the sound of an ambulance screaming through the night. People began to chatter nervously.

"Oh, my God! Victor!" Natasha cried. She turned and raced for the stairs. She was stopped by Garibaldi, with whom she argued. But this time, Garibaldi had apparently been given strict instructions by Kozak himself.

The wailing sirens stopped.

Natasha kept arguing with Garibaldi. Ivan was coming to join her, a strange look on his face. Was he frowning…or was that a look of satisfaction?

No one was near Jasmine at that moment. She heard a soft whisper at her ear.

Dean Jenkins was standing just behind her. "Jacob is with Kozak. They're heading to the hospital. Word will be out that he collapsed and that they're afraid of a heart attack."

Jasmine let him know she had heard him, nodding slightly, watching along with the others. She moved away from him. As she did so, she felt her phone vibrate in her pocket. She quickly made her way close to the bar, behind a structural beam, and answered it, halfway expecting Jacob.

But it wasn't Jacob.

"Jasmine!"

It was Kari Anderson.

"Jasmine, I need to tell you—"

"Kari, what? Kari?"

Jasmine looked at her phone; the call had ended. The line was dead.

"So, I will die. Or I will go to prison for the rest of my life," Kozak said, sighing softly. He shrugged. He was lying in the back of an ambulance. Comfortable.

It was a real ambulance. But they weren't real paramedics manning the vehicle, though they would really take Kozak to the hospital, where he would really be admitted.

Jacob had feared that Natasha or Ivan might have made their way upstairs before he'd managed to get Kozak out, but the ambulance had arrived just in time—and Kozak had been shoved right in and the vehicle had taken off into the night. Within moments of closing the ambulance doors, Jacob had revealed to him that he was FBI.

"Victor, the whole operation has to go down," Jacob told him. "I'm sure if you give the district attorney any help you can, he'll make the best arrangements possible."

"I can give you cartels. Names of the men who come and go with drugs and drug money."

"I'm not the DA," Jacob said.

"And I discovered that I do want to live, however long that may be," Kozak told him. He sighed. "My friend, will you do one thing for me?"

"This will be out of my hands now, Victor."

But Victor smiled. "This is a small thing. Before I am locked away, will you see to it that I get just one more…"

"One more what?"

"Shot of my good vodka!"

"I will do my best, Victor. I'm sure you have an attorney, and… I don't know. But for now, your best service is to give us the men who did put those bodies in the oil drums and who left the headless men in the Everglades."

"They want me dead."

"All the more reason we need anything you have to find out just who is calling the shots."

Jacob felt his phone vibrating in his pocket.

Jasmine? She had saved the night, somehow suspecting there might be poison in the vodka. But her cover might be jeopardized…

He answered the phone quickly.

It was Dean Jenkins. "She's gone after Connor, Jacob. Your detective associate."

"What? How? When?"

"The commotion started with the siren. She disappeared. And she saw Kari take off after Connor. We have a man on him, of course, and I'm on my way out, but—"

Jacob leaped up and hurried to the front of the ambulance. "Stop, let me out—quickly!" he said.

"Yes, sir. But—"

"Proceed, get him to a room, guards all around," Jacob said.

"Will do," the driver promised.

The ambulance jerked to a halt. Jacob jumped out and began to run. He had blocks to run, blocks filled with tourists, diners, children…

But at least Connor's apartment was north of the club. At least...

Jasmine was a cop; a good cop. She'd be all right. She'd think it out.

She was also emotional. She was afraid Mary had disappeared because Connor had done something horrible to her. Afraid that same horrible thing might happen to Kari...

"Hey!" a man protested.

Jacob just nudged past him and quickened his pace.

THANKS TO DEAN JENKINS, Jorge and all the other police and agents working the case, Jasmine knew where to go. Connor's room. She knew the street, the hotel complex and the number.

Naturally, it was on a side street—one that was poorly lit, for the beach. One that was a bit austere, where the rich came to stay, unburdened by the noise and ruckus of the average working-man tourist.

She ran up to the building. She could see the lobby through the plate-glass windows that surrounded the handsome interior. It was an old deco place redone—velvet upholstered chairs and a check-in reception that wasn't a counter but a desk. She could see a man with a newspaper in the lobby, watching the door.

FBI. The man watching Donald McPherson Connor? If so, he was nowhere near close enough.

Jasmine hesitated, taking a deep breath. One more time—one more try.

She pulled out her cell and dialed Kari's number. It rang once and went straight to voice mail.

She pocketed her phone and tried for a regal and nonchalant manner. She waited for the clerk to walk back into the office behind the desk.

Then she sashayed through as if she belonged there, despite her elaborate if dignified waitress uniform. She didn't know the man with the newspaper; he didn't know her. She offered him a brilliant smile and sauntered on through to the elevator.

She realized, in the elevator, that Connor had taken the penthouse; a floor all to himself. She was surprised when the elevator let her choose the top floor without any additional security.

The doors opened into a charming vestibule, rather than a hallway. It was as if she had arrived at someone's grand house. Handsome double doors led into the apartment itself.

She tried knocking, her heart beating a thousand drums a second. It would be illegal for her just to enter. She certainly couldn't force it open.

She waited…and no one came. The door might well be unlocked in such a building—in a good neighborhood, with security in the lobby.

And if she said she entered because she thought she heard a cry…

Just as Jasmine reached for the handle, the door opened.

Connor stood there, a gun in his hand.

"Ah, Jasmine," he said. "We've been waiting for you."

AS HE RAN, Jacob envisioned every manner of horror. His breath was coming hard; his calves were burning.

He knew he had made the right choice, running. It was the weekend on the beach, cars were bumper-to-bumper. For some reason there was an element of local society who thought it was cool to drive down Collins Avenue and show off their cars, some elegant, some souped-up, some convertibles, and some…just cars. Some with music blaring, and some discreetly quiet.

He was moving far faster than the cars.

And still…

He pictured Jasmine, bursting in on Connor. And Connor, ready for her, shots blazing before she could enter the room; Jasmine shooting back, maybe even taking the man down, as well. Injuring him, maybe killing him, but then lying there in a pool of blood, dark hair streaming through it, almost blue-black in contrast to the color of blood, eyes brilliant emerald as she stared into the night, and yet…sightless.

He had to stop thinking that way. He wasn't prone to panic; he'd have never survived his past.

His phone rang; he answered it anxiously, still running. It was Dean Jenkins.

"Natasha, Ivan, and the trio have headed to the hospital. I was just escorted out of the club. It went into lockdown. I found a place behind a dumpster by the cars. They all left together in the limo."

"Thanks. But no one goes in to see Kozak. They can be herded into a waiting room. They can't be near him. They can't know he's not really poisoned."

"We've got a 'doctor' ready to talk to them. As far as they'll know, Kozak is being airlifted to a trauma center where they're fighting to save his life."

"Thanks, Jenkins."

"Anything on your end yet?"

Apparently, Jenkins couldn't hear the way that he was panting. Just one more corner...

"Almost there."

He turned the corner and saw Connor's building, grand touches of Mediterranean-style along with the fine art deco architecture.

He ran through protocol in his mind—there was no right way to burst in on the man. This was a small part of what was going on; they didn't know who had killed Josef, who had tried to kill Kozak. The operation was in a crisis situation at the moment—and he needed to keep his cover.

He ran to the front, stopped briefly for a long breath and to gather his composure. He saw the agent with his newspaper—and the tiny dolphin tie tack that identified him. A clerk in a handsome suit sat at the desk.

There was no time; Jacob entered the lobby,

headed over to the man he'd never met, and greeted him. "Henry, how are you doing?"

"Great—fine fishing today. The kids come in tomorrow. We're going to take them over to Key Biscayne to see the lighthouse and then back to the Seaquarium—let them swim with some dolphins."

"Sounds like a plan. I've done the dolphin thing myself..." Jacob watched as the clerk headed to a back room. "How long?"

"Connor—just twenty minutes or so. Kari Anderson—fifteen. And then, another woman, just a matter of minutes."

Minutes...

Jacob headed for the elevator. It only took seconds for a bullet to find its mark. But as he reached the elevator, he realized the other agent had leaped to his feet to join him.

"I'm here now," Jacob said. "If I need backup, you'll know. If I'm not down—"

"Wait, there's just something you need to hear first," the agent said.

CONNOR NEVER HAD a chance to use his weapon.

Jasmine judged her distance—and the awkward way the man was holding the gun. She ducked low and took a flying leap at him, catching his legs, toppling him.

She'd been right; he was no gunslinger himself; he was completely inept. His gun went flying and he let out a yelp that made him sound like a wounded kitten.

She straddled him, pinning him down. "Where's Kari? What have you done with her?"

"What have I done with her?" He seemed stunned.

"You bastard, what have you done with her?"

It would be unethical, but…she was still playing a role. She'd taken him, and she meant to get the truth from him, beat it out of him if she had to. She could get away with this—one high-class escort worried about another, attacking a man…

But just as she was about to deliver a good right to his jaw, she heard her name called.

She looked up.

Kari was standing in the archway to the next room.

At the same time, she felt strong arms wrap around her waist, drawing her off of Connor. She twisted and fought and turned—

Jacob!

Jacob, stopping her, when she had the man down… "Let me go!" she demanded furiously.

"Jasmine, Jasmine, it's all right, you don't understand!" Kari cried. She rushed over to Connor, going down on her knees and trying to help the man up.

Astonished, Jasmine turned to Jacob. "What in God's name is happening?" she demanded, wrenching free from him. "Has everyone gone mad?"

Jacob turned and closed and locked the door and then looked at her.

For one moment, she felt extreme panic. Were they all in on it? Was Jacob a turncoat, had he somehow tricked the federal government, was this all…?

No! She believed in him, she knew him, knew this couldn't be.

"I admit, I don't fully know myself," Jacob said. "But we need to give Mr. Connor a chance to explain."

Connor was up on his feet, standing next to Kari—who was protectively holding his arm. "What is going on?" Connor asked.

"You first," Jacob told him.

"I'm just a citizen," Connor said. "Trying to…do the right thing."

Kari spoke up then, passionately. "Donald's daughter came to Miami Beach and wound up modeling with the group." She let out a long breath. "She was found dead on the beach. Drug overdose."

"I hire them to get them out," Connor whispered.

"But…but…" Jasmine began.

"Nan, my daughter, talked to me. She was frightened. She said that she couldn't forget what she had seen, and she was afraid that someone knew she knew about the cocaine, and…then she was found dead. She wasn't an addict. She didn't do drugs. I called the police—there was an investigation, and it went nowhere. The officers tried, but Nan wasn't found anywhere near the club, she'd been out with friends, she'd said she was leaving, and… they killed her. I know they killed her. And I couldn't get justice, so—"

"Donald made arrangements for me to get away—far away. Hide out, and then start over," Kari said softly. "I wanted to get ahead so badly, be rich and famous…be loved. I did things I'm not proud of. And I couldn't see any way out. But... Donald is a savior!"

"I need some kind of proof," Jacob said. "And if this is all true, Mr. Connor, I am so sorry and, of course, so grateful, and you're a fool, as well. You're risking your own life."

"My life does not matter so much anymore," Connor said flatly. "I have proof—our airline tickets. I was taking Kari to London tonight and then on to Yorkshire, to settle her with my family there."

Jasmine stared at them all, incredulous. And then it hit her. Connor's daughter...dead.

"Mary," she murmured.

"Mary?" Connor said. "Mary Ahearn?"

Jasmine stared at him.

Connor smiled. "Lovely young woman. She tried to help me find out which one of those horrible people was responsible for Nan's death. She tried to find out what was going on."

"So, you gave her a death sentence, too," Jasmine whispered.

He shook his head, looking a bit confused but still smiling. "Mary is alive and well. She's at my estate in Yorkshire, happily working on a play she's been longing to write. Of course, she'd love to be acting, and she's very fond of British theater, so she just might want to stay on. I asked her not to contact anyone from her former life until we were sure she was safe."

Jasmine would have fallen over. She felt Jacob's strength as his arms came around her.

He was staring across the room at Connor. "We will have to verify your information. And I hope you're telling the truth. If so, I swear to you, we will get justice for your daughter. I'm setting you up with an agent to get safely out of the country. I don't think you'll be bothered tonight—there's too much else going on right now."

"Why did you call me? Why did you hang up?" Jasmine demanded of Kari.

"My—my phone died! I figured I'd call you and let you know I was leaving as soon as possible," Kari said. "And then we were getting my things, and Donald promised he'd come back and get you out, but he thought you were safe, that Jacob might be a criminal, but he'd be watching over you and then somehow, he'd get to you and—I'm so sorry!"

"One thing, please," Connor said.

"What?" Jacob demanded.

"Who the hell are you people?" Connor asked.

Chapter Twelve

It felt odd that it had just been that afternoon that Josef Smirnoff had been lain to rest. The ceremony at the club had taken place, and Jacob had ushered Kozak out in an ambulance, pretending the man was at death's door.

While Jacob and Jasmine were at Connor's suite, Kozak had gone into the hospital—and then out another door. He had immediately been ushered out to a FBI facility out west in Miami, in a little area with scores of ranch houses built in the 1970s, heading west off the canal that bordered the Tamiami Trail all the way across the south end of the peninsula to Naples, Florida.

Agents watching the hospitals—the beach hospital where Kozak had first been taken and the county hospital with the trauma center where he'd supposedly been brought later—

had kept up with Jacob; Jasmine had been in touch with the MDPD who had in turn been in touch with the Miami Beach department, and everyone was on alert in case another attempt was made on the life of their new informant.

The entire inner core of Kozak's circle had arrived at the beach hospital, only to be assured that everything was being done, but that no one could see Victor Kozak. They had left together, but now Ivan and Natasha were back at the club with only Antonovich to watch over the doors. Natasha had been a mess, so Jasmine and Jacob were told—and had to be sedated when she was told that Kozak was on the verge of death.

Jacob had received many calls from both Ivan and Natasha, but he had told them both that he also had been kicked out of the hospital for having grown too insistent on seeing a man when an intensive care crew was busy trying to save him.

It was well after midnight by the time Donald McPherson Connor and Kari Anderson had been escorted to the airport—and safely onto their plane. Jasmine had gone from being ready to rip the man's throat out to being his best friend—they'd wound up talking and talking.

Kari had told her she'd wanted to say more, but she couldn't. She'd been afraid of what Jasmine might say or do, not at all certain that Jacob wasn't on the rise through the gang—or that Jasmine wasn't already completely beneath his control.

Connor had spoken about his own grief and then about dealing with it in the most constructive way he could.

"You really took chances," Jacob had told him.

"Not so much. I wasn't in on anything. I was just a client. Not someone making money—I was someone giving them money." He paused and shrugged. "And money is something I have. But it means nothing when you don't have the ones you love to share it with."

Jacob had to admit, he was a bit in awe of the man himself. Grief and loss often destroyed the loving survivors; Connor had channeled his resources and himself into saving others.

Naturally, Jacob hadn't immediately trusted what he heard, but with the information Connor gave him, the FBI offices were able to verify his story. The man did own a huge estate in Yorkshire. In truth, he had a title. He also held dual citizenship and spent as much time in the

States—recently in the pursuit of saving the lives of young women—as in Great Britain.

And so it was two in the morning when Jacob and Jasmine returned to her apartment. She didn't seem the least bit tired. She was keyed up and alive, filled with energy.

"She's all right, Jacob! Mary is fine. She's in England...and I've been so, so afraid!"

He was sitting on the sofa, wiped out. She'd been all but flying around the room. In her happiness, that flight took her to fall down on his lap, sweeping her arms around him, her smile bright and her eyes as dazzling an emerald as could ever be imagined.

Her touch removed a great deal of his own exhaustion.

"She's alive, and you have to meet her. Oh, Jacob, to think I wanted to skin that man alive, that I thought he was part of..." Her voice trailed off and she frowned.

"What?" he asked, reaching out to stroke back a long lock of her hair.

"We're no closer to the truth. Nan Connor was afraid because she was a witness to a huge cocaine deal. But we don't know who saw her, and there's no way we can find out. We're pretending that Kozak is dying, but none of the gang has risen up to try to take over."

"Jasmine, as far as I know, they wouldn't dare do so. They don't believe that Kozak is dead as of yet, and they won't dare play their cards until they do."

"Where do we go from here?"

"Everything is in motion. I don't even call the shots from here on out. I'll go out tomorrow to interrogate Kozak, but it's going to be up to men with much higher positions than mine to determine what our next steps are. Kozak was grateful just to be alive." He paused, looking at her. "That was an amazing save tonight— the poison in the vodka. How did you know?"

"When he talked about his special reserve, it occurred to me that he'd be the only one drinking it. I'd hoped I'd find out who had brought the bottle and handed it to the bartender, but the guy was from the catering company and he said the bar had been set up when he got there, with the instructions that the special reserve stuff was for Kozak and Kozak only."

"Impressive." He smiled, watching her eyes. "You are a veritable beast. I thought you were going to rip Connor's head off. We're lucky you didn't shoot. He had a gun, right? You need to slow down—you could have gotten yourself killed."

"I could see he didn't know what he was doing with the gun," Jasmine said. Then she frowned. "How did you know that he wasn't going to kill anyone?"

"The agent watching him, Special Agent Daubs, Miami Criminal Division. He'd overheard Connor and Kari talking. And he watched them. Said he was a pretty good judge of men, and I guess he was."

"I'm glad," Jasmine said softly.

"So now, once again, we wait. Tomorrow, I'll spend some time out with Kozak. And you and Jorge and others will be on the beach, waiting, ready to move if anything does break—play your part. But don't go anywhere near the club."

"I still have my uniform."

"If they call you, let me know right away. And for now—"

"Tonight?" she asked seriously.

"Sleep would be on the agenda."

"Ah, yes, sleep."

"Perhaps some rigorous exercise to speed the process," he suggested.

"We are still playing roles," she murmured.

"Jorge did say we were method actors."

"We can always work on method," she whispered.

Jacob wondered vaguely what it was about a special woman, that her slightest whisper, the nuance in her words, her lightest touch, could awaken everything in a man. There was no one in the world anything like her, he thought.

She stood, reaching for his hand. He rose, smiling. In the bedroom, they both saw to their weapons first. They barely touched, shedding their clothing in a hurry.

He went down on the bed, patting the mattress, and for a moment, she stood, sleek and stunning as a silhouette in the pale light from the hallway. She moved with grace, coming to him, and then she was next to him, in his arms, and if anything, they were more frantic that night to touch and to tease and to taste one another. To make love.

Later, when they should have been drifting off to sleep, she rose up on an elbow, looking at him, empathy in the ever-brilliant sheen of her eyes. "Forgive me, but…"

He knew what she wanted to know. So, he told her about growing up in Miami at first and moving to New York. Falling in love with Sabrina in high school, college, the service…

"Going off to the Middle East," he said. "She was always so worried about me. And she was vibrant. Full of life. We were happy. I'd done my service and I knew I wanted to head into the FBI Academy. I was certain I'd make it. We never thought… Well, she was diagnosed, and three months later, she was gone."

"I am so, so sorry."

"It was over ten years ago now," he told her, rolling to better see her face, stroke her cheek. "But you…hmm. Can't figure how you manage to be unattached. Of course, Jorge told me that you do have a tendency to shut a guy down before he can ask you out."

"Jorge talks way too much."

He laughed softly and pulled her into his arms. "That's all right," he told her. "I'm not an easy man to shut down."

She grinned, indicating their positions. "I didn't try very hard to shut you down."

He laughed and she was in his arms again.

SHE WAS NO good at waiting. She would never make it full time in undercover work.

Jasmine actually tried to sleep after Jacob

left. His phone had rung far too early, letting him know that a car was coming to take him to the safe house where Kozak was being guarded. But sleep was impossible. She made coffee, washed and dried her hair and was tempted to try to do her own nails, since she had a rare moment of downtime. She reminded herself how incredibly happy she was—how grateful.

Mary was fine, alive and well. Kari was fine, too. They'd met a man who was trying to prevent future wrongs.

Still, someone within the gang was truly cold-blooded. At least eight people were dead because of the person within who considered murder to be a stepping-stone to criminal power.

If only Jacob were there to bounce her theories off of. They worked well together. Even when they were just playing roles. But the roles had become so much more. She'd found someone who seemed to really care about her, who could be with her, for all that she was, for what she did.

These roles would come to an end. That didn't mean they had to stop seeing each other, but her life, her work, was here. And his life and work were in New York.

It was foolish to think about the future. In the middle of this, she couldn't even be certain that either of them had a future. She had faith in herself and faith in him and all their colleagues—but no one entered into law enforcement without recognizing the dangers.

Worrying about the future was not helping her keep from crawling up the walls.

She couldn't call a friend and go out. She was still undercover. And Jacob had told her not to go near the club.

She was on her third cup of coffee when she realized that she could call Jorge. She was so antsy she'd probably annoy him, but Jorge never seemed to mind. As the thought occurred to her, she felt her phone ring.

"Jorge!"

"Hey, gorgeous, whatcha doing?"

"I was about to call you. I'm waiting. Doing what I was told to do. Climbing the walls. Being such a desperate cop I'm ready to watch a marathon of *Desperate Housewives* with you."

"Well, I have a reprieve for you. I'm on my

way. All sanctioned. Come out to the corner. I'll be by for you."

"Perfect. Jeans okay?"

"Jeans and sneakers. Great. See you in five minutes."

"This is cleared with Captain Lorenzo— and the FBI?"

"Yeah, we're supposed to be heading to a music venue controlled by the gang. Top groups. Acting like normal people. Waiting like the rest of the folks around us, finding out if Kozak is going to make it. Gauging their reactions."

"Okay!" Jasmine rang off and shoved her phone into her cross-body handbag. She hurried out, carefully locking her apartment, all but running by the bathers out by the pool, aware of the bright sun and the waving palms.

A car pulled over to the curb; it wasn't a car she knew, but an impressive SUV. FBI issue for work down here?

Jorge rolled down the passenger-side window. "Hop in!" he said cheerfully.

"Where did you get the car?" she asked.

"City of Miami Beach," he said. He was smiling broadly, but she frowned. Something about him didn't seem quite right.

But while she and Jorge might never have discussed their personal lives, they were solid working partners. They always had one another's back. He would die for her...

It wasn't until she was inext to the car that she realized Jorge wasn't alone in the car.

There was a man in the back, but Jasmine's focus went to the fact that he had the business edge of a serious knife against the throat of a woman he'd shoved down in the seat. The young woman was trying desperately hard not to snuffle or cry out, with that blade so close to her artery.

It was Helen Lee, the sweet and lovely young woman with whom she and Kari had shared the runway.

Helen was absolutely terrified.

The man with the knife smiled. She was not entirely surprised to see who it was.

"Welcome, Jasmine. Now, Jorge, drive. And no tricks, no running us off the road. You wouldn't want my hand to slip. You wouldn't want to see this blade slice right through Helen's throat, would you? Jorge—drive. Now. Jasmine, smile. Please. It will keep my hand so much steadier."

Jasmine's gun was in her purse, but she

couldn't reach for it then. So was her phone. She believed that the man would slit Helen's throat.

As she slid into the car, she kept her bag clutched tightly in her hands.

FROM THE OUTSIDE, it looked like any other house. It sat off 122nd Avenue and Southwest Eighth Street—the Tamiami Trail there and farther west—or Calle Ocho when you headed way back east toward downtown Miami.

Built in the 1970s, it was a ranch-style home like many of the others surrounding them. It had a large lot, but so did several other houses in the area. This house, however, had a little gazebo out front, covered with vines—a fine place for an agent to keep guard—and a large garage and a few storage sheds out back.

The living room was like any other living room. It had a sofa and some plush chairs and a stereo system and a large-screen TV. The windows were all barred—but then, so were many of the other houses in the area, a deterrent to would-be burglars.

Just like so many other houses, there were signs on the fence that warned Beware of Dogs, and the dogs were the kind for which people should be wary. Signs also warned about the house being protected by a local security company, one used by many of the other residents of the area.

There was a kitchen, usually well stocked. There was a well-appointed gym, but then again, other people had home gyms. A dining room sat between the living room and the kitchen. The house boasted four bedrooms.

One of those bedrooms had no bed.

It had a table and chairs, and it was where guests were often required to engage in conversation with those who had brought them here.

Kozak sat in one chair. Jacob sat in another. Also at the table was Dean Jenkins—the man Josef Smirnoff had first approached in fear for his life.

One other man had joined them, Carl Merrill, a prosecutor from the United States Office of the Attorney General.

"As I told Jacob—before I realized how determined my would-be murderer was—I have never killed anyone," Kozak said.

"Your actions have resulted in the deaths of many," Merrill said.

"I can give you so much," Kozak told him. "But I must have a deal. I must."

"What is that you think you can give me? We've got you, head of an organized crime gang, and enough evidence of your activities to prosecute," Merrill asked.

"Names. I can give you the names of men who look squeaky-clean, who are working with the cartels out of South America. There are bigger fish than me in Miami."

"Victor," Jacob said, "you can't even give us the name of the man who wants you dead, who wants to take over the Deco Gang. Let's see—he's been working for you. And we know he forced a lethal dose of cocaine into a young woman who was a model for you. And he's likely responsible for at least three corpses in oil drums in Broward County and three headless corpses in the Everglades."

Kozak spun on him. "I don't kill. And I don't order executions!" he said angrily. "If I knew, could a murderer have come so close, would I have been about to drink poison?"

"Deals have yet to be made, Victor. We need help now. Who locked the door to the balcony on the day that Josef Smirnoff was killed?" Jacob asked.

"Josef." Kozak sighed. "I can't go to a federal prison…not in the general population. We had reputations. There are too many men who might think me guilty of crimes I did not commit. A man in my position does not deny violent acts to others of his kind. A reputation is everything. I let mine grow as it would."

Jenkins leaned forward. "Victor, let's start here. Did you know that Smirnoff contacted me?"

"No, I did not."

"Had he been acting nervous in any way?"

Kozak appeared to think about that and slowly shook his head. His voice was husky when he spoke. "If he was afraid, he would not have shown it anyway."

"Do you believe he suspected you?" Jacob asked.

"If so, he shouldn't have."

"Was he sleeping with Natasha—were they a real couple?"

Kozak hesitated on that one. "Yes, she was… strong. And good."

"So, you inherited Natasha along with the leadership," Jacob said. "She had the key to the balcony yesterday."

"There is only one key. She had it because I would not be present."

"Do you think it is Natasha who might be trying to kill you? Would she be hard enough to have one of her girls killed—and to order the execution of those men?"

Kozak smiled. "Natasha, she is a woman. But in business…this business? Natasha serves," he said softly.

Jacob had to wonder at that.

But Kozak was convinced of the truth of his words. He shook his head. "I don't know, I really don't know. As they say, keep your friends close, but your enemies closer. I have kept my people close. I don't know how they can be hiring these killers, desperate people."

There was a knock at the door. The agent who was the house's "owner" stepped in. "Special Agent Wolff, a word."

"Now?"

"Yes, sir. Now."

Jacob politely excused himself. Outside the room, he realized the agent was anxious.

"It's a call from Captain Lorenzo, sir, MDPD. Our men on the beach were following a car out of the club, but they lost them on the causeway. I—"

He stopped talking and handed Jacob the phone.

The man on the line quickly, tersely, identified himself as Captain Mac Lorenzo.

"I don't know how she did it, but Jasmine managed to contact this number and leave her phone on. She's in a car—they're headed west somewhere. Jorge is driving, Jasmine is in the front. There's a man in back, and from what I can hear, he's taking them somewhere. It sounds as if they're headed for an execution. We've got men on it, but they keep losing them. I've already asked the Feds to hop on it as quickly as possible, but you were close to that group. I'm hoping you might know where they're being taken."

Jacob froze for a split second; he felt as if the life had been stripped out of him.

"I need the exact location those headless bodies were found," Jacob said. "Speak fast, I'm already moving. And keep the others back. If the killer feels cornered, he'll kill whoever he has close out of spite. Get me backup, but keep the backup back."

Lorenzo kept talking. Before he finished another sentence, Jacob was in a car and heading west down the Tamiami Trail.

"NOT SO SLOW that the police notice us. There's no need to risk another of the city's finest."

Hearing the voice of the man in the back, Jorge cast a quick glance toward Jasmine. His eyes were filled with agony. She knew how he felt.

A quick look in back assured her there was already a fine line of blood creating a jagged necklace along Helen Lee's throat.

Jasmine and Jorge would both fight, play for time, for the life of another, as long as they were both still breathing.

There was no way to let him know she'd gotten her hand into her purse, and that she was pretty sure she'd hit the number one; a priority call that would hit the phone Lorenzo had just for communication with her.

But would Lorenzo know where they were going? How could he know when she didn't know?

West. They were headed west. Jorge was driving as slowly as he could reasonably manage without drawing the man's ire or suspicion.

He was in no rush to bring them to their destination. They were off the beach now, across the causeway on a long, long drive that seemed to be taking them out to the Everglades.

It was a land a few of the hardiest knew well, where airboat rides could be found, where the Miccosukee kept a restaurant and reservation lands, where visitors could find out about their lives and their pasts.

A place where, no matter how many hearty souls worked and even lived, there were acres upon acres that was nothing but wetland, part of the great "river of grass," filled with water moccasins and alligators, even pythons and boas.

"To the Everglades," she said aloud, as they whipped past the Miccosukee casino.

She turned around and stared at Ivan Petrov.

"You want to kill Jorge and me. Why?"

He eyed her coldly and then smiled. "I don't believe that Kozak is dead. He's the one who brought Marensky in. You did something with his drink. Marensky called the ambulance, and now…now they do not report that Kozak is dead."

"Whatever your argument with me, why Helen?" she asked.

His smiled deepened. "She happened to be there," he said.

Ivan Petrov. They should have figured; they had looked at Kozak, at Natasha, at the goons... They would have gotten to Ivan. He was never off the list.

"I need some guarantee you're going to keep Helen alive," Jasmine said. "Then Jorge and I will do as you ask."

"You are with the government," Petrov said.

"I swear to you, I am not an FBI agent. Neither is Jorge."

"Then you are trying to take the lead, playing up to Kozak. Well, they have cold feet. The enterprise will never be what it should be under Kozak. He is a weakling—he doesn't know how to remove what festers among us. Drive, Jorge. And turn around, Miss Jasmine."

The casino was behind them. Minutes were counting down. They were coming up to Shark Valley when Petrov told Jorge to slow the car down.

He couldn't be going to Shark Valley! There were trails and bike paths, tourists and rangers all about. Unless he meant to kill anyone in his way.

They didn't turn into Shark Valley. They

passed the entrance, and the Miccosukee restaurant to the right on the road.

Then suddenly, Kozak said, "Here."

Here? She knew of no road here...

"Now!" Petrov commanded.

Helen let out a scream as the knife pierced her flesh.

Jorge turned.

JACOB WAS MET by Mickey Cypress of the Miccosukee Police. The man was in his early forties, lean, bronze and no-nonsense. He'd been waiting for Jacob right outside the entrance to Shark Valley.

"You don't want to go exactly where the bodies were found," he told Jacob. "The Everglades is literally a river, and the bodies were carried until they were snagged by the mangrove roots." He had a map out on his phone and he pointed to a spot that seemed to be just beyond a canal where they stood.

Jacob glanced at the map. Suddenly, two giant male alligators went into some kind of a battle in the canal.

"Leave them alone, completely alone," Cypress told him. "There's a marshy trail we can take through here, and a small hammock.

That's where I think we'll find their killing grounds. There was no road there before, but some fairly solid ground. I think they created their own way."

Cars drove up next to them. Men in suits got out—the backup.

Cypress looked at him. They were probably good agents; they just didn't look ready for a trek into the water and marshy land.

"Special Agent Wolff!" one of them called.

Jacob looked at Cypress.

"I'm with you," Cypress said. "Um, if you're trying for stealth…"

Jacob nodded and headed back to the agent calling to him. He asked him to hold their position and keep a line of contact open. He walked back to Cypress.

The local cop told him, "Trust me, I know how to get there. I was the first on call when the bodies were found. I've been on this."

"I trust you," Jacob assured him. "We need to hurry. I got after them right away, but they still had a head start."

"Then we move."

Cypress started over a small land bridge, just feet from the male alligators defending their turf. Water came cascading over them from a massive flip of a tail.

They kept walking.

Ivan Petrov had his knife—and a gun on his belt. He kept the knife at Helen's throat.

Jasmine clung to her purse.

"Drop it!" Petrov commanded. His knife moved ever so slightly.

Helen gulped out a cry. Tears were streaming down her face—silent tears. She tried not to sob and stared at Jasmine—any movement would cause a great chafe of the knife against her throat. Her eyes were both imploring and hopeless.

"Go!" Petrov commanded. Jorge walked ahead; Jasmine behind him. He sheathed the knife and drew his gun.

"I don't understand, Ivan. Who were the people in the oil drums?" Jasmine asked.

"Well, I will tell you," Petrov said. "The first, his name was Terry Meyers. He thought he should manage the club—and the women. That was long ago, when Smirnoff had barely begun to settle into South Florida. Smirnoff was, in fact, surprised when Meyers failed to arrive for a meeting. The second, well, he failed to show with a payment. He made me look bad. You can't deal with people who don't deliver on goods or who don't make their payments. It's bad for business if you don't follow through. Same deal for the third loser."

"The three who weren't in the drums," she said. "They were the ones who killed Josef."

"Yes, actually, they were very good. I was sorry to see them go. But you see, they couldn't live. If they had been apprehended, well... I did hire them personally."

"You admired them so much, you beheaded them," Jasmine murmured.

Jorge glanced back at her; she was doing the right thing, keeping him talking. There were two of them. They could survive this. They had to get Helen in a safe position, and then they could rush Petrov—he couldn't shoot them both at the same time.

But they had to get Helen away from him first.

Jorge suddenly stopped, letting out a shout.

"Move!" Petrov commanded.

"There's a gator ahead in the path," Jorge said, falling back by Jasmine.

"That's fine," Petrov said, dragging Helen around and waving his gun at the small gator on the trail. "We're almost there." He fired the gun toward the gator. The creature moved off into the surrounding bracken.

There was some kind of a structure there, a broken-down shack, a remnant, Jasmine thought, from the time when various Florida hunters had come out and kept little camps.

It was now or never—Petrov had just fired the gun, he was looking away, he was holding Helen, but the gun wasn't directly at her throat.

Jasmine didn't let out a sound; she made a silent leap for the man.

She bore him down to the ground. Helen slipped free, screaming hysterically. She began to run back in the direction from which they had come, screaming all the while.

Petrov's gun hand was flailing; in a second, the barrel would be aiming at Jasmine's face.

But Jorge was there, stomping on the man's wrist, kicking at the gun. It went flying into a gator hole, filled high with water.

But Petrov wasn't going down easily. He caught Jasmine and flipped her down to the muddy earth.

Jorge kicked his head.

Petrov had the knife on his belt now; Jasmine went for it. Seizing it from Petrov, she sliced his hand. He cried out as blood gushed.

And then, a gunshot fired. They all went still.

The knife still tightly in her grip, Jasmine turned to the sound.

Standing casually now before the rotting wood of the old shack was Natasha. She shook her head.

"Men. They are worthless, eh? They continually think they are in charge, and they have no idea. Ivan! A silly girl and these two. You have a gun, you have a knife, and they best you. What would you have done without me, Ivan?"

She shook her head again at Ivan, but then smiled at Jasmine. "Yes, you are one who knows how to manipulate a man, eh? It's the only way, until you have seized the position of real power. And then they will bow down before you, and they will become your toys, and you will command them. It's a pity you must die. It will be hard for me... Oh, maybe not so hard, because now Ivan and I will have to crawl through this wretched swamp looking for that silly Helen. If she doesn't kill herself first. Maybe it will not be so hard. I will kill your friend first, so you can watch him die, and he will not have to watch you die? How is that?"

"I should have known you were the one with ice-cold blood running in your veins—right from the beginning," Jasmine said.

Natasha shrugged. "Me? I am not so much the killer. I like others to do the killing."

"And then you kill the killers."

Natasha smiled. "Ivan killed the killers. I simply cut off their hands and their heads… and fed them to the swamp. Enough talk." She took aim.

But Natasha couldn't have known what hit her.

He came from behind. His arm came down on hers and Natasha screamed with shock and pain as she lost her grip on the gun, as she was tackled to the ground.

Jasmine stared.

Jacob was there. Impossibly, Jacob was there. He'd slipped around silently from behind the hut, and he was now reading Natasha her rights and handcuffing her, heedless of the fact that he was on her back and pressing her face into the mud.

He looked at Jasmine, his recitation breaking. He nodded toward Petrov, who was trying to turn and escape.

Jasmine turned to Petrov, but another man—never before sensed nor seen—went sliding past her.

"Not to worry. I've got that one."

Jacob yanked Natasha to her feet. He spoke into his phone. Jasmine and Jorge were still just standing there, incredulous to be alive, when men—a little ridiculously dressed in fine blue suits and leather loafers—came running through the brush.

"Got her, sir," one of them said to Jacob, taking Natasha. He was young, younger than Jasmine. A brand-new agent, she thought, but ready to do whatever was asked of him, including running through a swampy, mucky river in his office attire.

He was gone; Natasha was dragged away. And then they heard shouts; Ivan had been apprehended, as well.

"Helen—Helen Lee is running through the swamp," Jasmine called out, her voice echoing through the mangroves and pines.

One of the agents came back. "No, ma'am, we've got her. She's fine. A little scratched up and still hysterical, but…we've got her. She's going to be okay."

"Hey, I'm coming with you," Jorge said. "She knows me. I'll get her calmed down."

And then, for a moment, Jasmine and Jacob were standing there alone. A large white crane swooped in and settled down near them, seeing a fish in the shallow gator holes that surrounded them on the small hammock.

Slowly, Jasmine smiled. "Your timing is impeccable."

He let out a long soft sigh, and then he grinned. "So I've been told."

She raced across the mud and the muck that separated them and threw herself into his arms. And they indulged in one long kiss, both shaking.

"You are kick-ass," he told her.

"But not even a kick-ass can work alone," she whispered. "You saved our lives."

"Only because you were doing a good enough job saving your own life," he assured her. "Lord, help me, this may be ridiculous, but I think I love you."

"This may be more ridiculous," she said.

"What?"

"I know I love you!" she told him.

"Special Agent Wolff? Detective?" They were being summoned.

Hand in hand, they started back along the path. "Paperwork," Jacob murmured.

"And then?" she asked.

He wiped a spot of mud off her face. "Showers," he said. "Definitely showers."

She smiled and he paused just one more minute, turning her to him.

"And then," he said, blue eyes dazzling down on her, "then figuring out our lives. If that's all right with you, of course."

She rose on her toes and lightly kissed his lips.

She could have done much, much more, but others were waiting—and there were some very large predators near them. The human ones might be down, but while she wasn't afraid of the creatures here, she wasn't stupid enough to get in their way either.

She broke the kiss and looked into his clear eyes. "It's all right with me."

Epilogue

The woman hurrying toward him along the long stone path over the castle's moat was truly one of the most stunning creatures Jacob Wolff had ever seen. His initial opinion of Jasmine had never changed.

Her skin was pure bronze, as sleek and as dazzling as the deepest sunray. When she smiled at him, he could see that her eyes were light. Green, he knew, an emerald green, and a sharp contrast to her skin. She had amazing hair, long and so shimmering that it was as close to pure black as it was possible to be; so dark it almost had a glint of violet. She was long-legged, lean and yet exquisitely shaped, even in jeans, sweater, boots and a parka.

She didn't pause when she met him. She threw her arms around him and leaped up so he had to catch her, and laughed as he spun with her in the rising sunlight that did little to dispel the chill of the damp day. No one saw them.

Donald McPherson Connor's "estate" had proved to be a castle. Small, admittedly, but *a bit of an historic home*, as Donald called it, and far out in the countryside of northern England.

"Best vacation ever!" she told him, sliding down to stand.

He looked behind her. They were no longer alone.

He'd headed out for a walk on the grounds right after morning coffee; Jasmine had stayed behind to wait for Mary and Jorge—the two had been in a lengthy discussion of just how cold it might get during the day, and throwing her hands up, Jasmine had indicated he should go ahead.

His hike had been serene. The countryside seemed to stretch endlessly, beautiful rolling land with horses and sheep and cattle.

He'd had vacation time built up—you couldn't just hop off to an amusement park or the mountains or the French Riviera in the middle of work when you were deep in an undercover operation. He felt this time off was well deserved, for himself and for Jasmine. It had been impossible for them to turn down Donald Connor's suggestion that they come to visit Mary.

They had a suite in the tiny castle. No windows facing a beach, but instead an arrow slit that looked out over a stretch of land that was misty and green. They had long nights together and days with amazing friends.

Jorge and Mary caught up with them. "Off to the theater, if you're sure you don't mind the walk," she said.

Mary was as gentle and sweet a woman as Jasmine had said, wide-eyed and kind, with blond hair as long as Jasmine's raven tresses. Mary had cried when she'd come to the airport to meet them; she'd been so sorry to have frightened Jasmine, to have put her in danger. But Donald had explained that he was just an ordinary citizen—he'd needed Mary to not say a word to anyone until she was safely out of the clutches of the Deco Gang. She'd been lucky to have an up-to-date passport.

Mary told them that Natasha had instructed her they had more escort work, and the intended client was a man she had seen come and go with different suitcases. She had suspected the man was part of their drug operation. And by then she knew that the girls weren't really models, that the so-called models were being prostituted, and that she just might not be able to do all of the things expected of her. And that if they suspected that she knew too much—or anything at all—she just might wind up dead.

Jasmine explained to her over and over again that it was all right—they'd put a stop to it all, and possibly saved many more lives.

Natasha had gone through people quickly. In her mind, so it seemed, people were as disposable as silverware or linens that were no longer needed.

There was, of course, a note of sadness to it all. They could do nothing for Donald's daughter; she was gone. But while he couldn't be happy, the man was grateful and satisfied. Her killers would find justice.

"A walk is great," Jacob assured her.

"Okay, so maybe these ugly shoes are good," Jorge said, slipping an arm around Mary's shoulders. The two of them moved slightly ahead. Mary began telling Jorge about the history of the area and how old the theater they were about to attend was.

Jasmine looked up at Jacob and smiled. "It's a children's play we're seeing, you know."

"Mary wrote it—I can't wait to see it. Donald will join us there?"

"Exactly," Jasmine said.

Mary suddenly stopped. She looked back, grinning. "Hey, I was talking to Donald this morning, earlier. He thinks you guys should have your wedding here."

Jasmine stopped dead. "Mary, we're visitors here. And we haven't—" she looked at Jacob, a flush rising to her cheeks "—we haven't even..."

Talked about marriage.

They had talked about everything else. A long-distance relationship seemed like half measures. But then, what to do? Jasmine loved the people with whom she worked, and she loved Miami. Jacob understood. They were looking into a transfer for him to the Miami office.

It had only been a few weeks since they'd survived the murder attempt in the Everglades; they'd been mulling over all possibilities in the meantime. And of course, finishing the endless paperwork, the United States Attorney General, the police, evidence, witnesses and everything else that went with the end of such a complicated case.

Kozak was going into witness protection; both Ivan and Natasha would be prosecuted for the murders they had committed. Victor Kozak had given the authorities all they needed to apprehend a number of the drug smugglers in Miami Beach, and information regarding them that might lead to solving many of the cold cases on file across Greater Miami.

Antonovich, Garibaldi and Suarez had worked for Kozak, and though they had faced stiff interrogations, they hadn't actually been proved guilty of any crimes. Jacob hoped that the three would find better employment.

Petrov still had a problem believing he was going down—he'd tried to throw everything on Natasha, but in turn, Natasha had tried to throw everything on him.

The man had been a fool, Jacob had told Jasmine, when they had been alone and curled together one night. He'd underestimated the power of a woman. And, smiling, he'd assured her, "That's something I never would do."

Now, Jacob grabbed her hand, forcing her to look at him. "I don't know—the wedding here. What do you think?"

"I..." Jasmine looked at him.

Jorge let out a sound of frustration. "Oh,

come on! You know there's going to be a wedding. Seriously, who else could either of you live with forever and ever, huh?"

He was right. You were very, very lucky in life when you found that one person who complemented you in every way.

Jacob looked into her eyes, so strong, so gentle, so giving… Dazzling.

He figured he could answer for both of them. "I don't really care where we get married. As long as we do. And I do need to get you all to New York. I have a friend—I've worked with him and the love of his life, and her family owns an Irish pub on Broadway. Her brother is also an actor and can score all kinds of theater tickets, Mary."

"New York—oh, I would love it! But first—a wedding in a castle. We'll let you do the honeymoon alone, and then an after-honeymoon in New York. Perfect!" Mary caught Jorge's hand and the two walked on ahead.

Jacob caught Jasmine's hand. He went down on a knee. "Detective Adair, will you marry me? In a castle, at the courthouse, Miami, New York…wherever? I cannot begin to imagine my life without you. It can be here, there or anywhere."

Jasmine came down on a knee, as well. "My dearest Special Agent Wolff, yes. Here, there, anywhere," she assured him. "I can't imagine my life ever again without you!"

He leaned forward, and they kissed. And kissed...

Until Jorge called back to them. "Hey! Time for that later. We're going to miss the play."

Laughing, Jasmine rose and pulled him to his feet. "The rest of our lives," she said.

"The rest of our lives," he agreed.

* * * * *

Get 4 FREE REWARDS!

We'll send you 2 FREE Books plus 2 FREE Mystery Gifts.

FREE
Value Over
$20

Both the **Romance** and **Suspense** collections feature compelling novels
written by many of today's best-selling authors.

YES! Please send me 2 FREE novels from the Essential Romance or
Essential Suspense Collection and my 2 FREE gifts (gifts are worth about
$10 retail). After receiving them, if I don't wish to receive any more books,
I can return the shipping statement marked "cancel." If I don't cancel, I will
receive 4 brand-new novels every month and be billed just $6.74 each in the
U.S. or $7.24 each in Canada. That's a savings of at least 16% off the cover
price. It's quite a bargain! Shipping and handling is just 50¢ per book in the
U.S. and 75¢ per book in Canada.* I understand that accepting the 2 free
books and gifts places me under no obligation to buy anything. I can always
return a shipment and cancel at any time. The free books and gifts are mine
to keep no matter what I decide.

Choose one: ☐ **Essential Romance**   ☐ **Essential Suspense**
                    (194/394 MDN GMY7)   (191/391 MDN GMY7)

Name (please print)

Address   Apt. #

City   State/Province   Zip/Postal Code

> Mail to the **Reader Service:**
> **IN U.S.A.:** P.O. Box 1341, Buffalo, NY 14240-8531
> **IN CANADA:** P.O. Box 603, Fort Erie, Ontario L2A 5X3

Want to try 2 free books from another series? Call 1-800-873-8635 or visit www.ReaderService.com.

READERSERVICE.COM

Manage your account online!

- Review your order history
- Manage your payments
- Update your address

*We've designed the
Reader Service website
just for you.*

Enjoy all the features!

- Discover new series available to you, and read excerpts from any series.
- Respond to mailings and special monthly offers.
- Browse the Bonus Bucks catalog and online-only exculsives.
- Share your feedback.

Visit us at:
ReaderService.com

RS16R